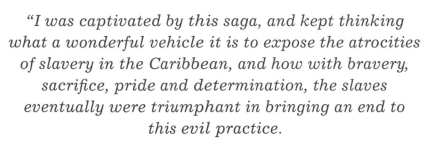
"I was captivated by this saga, and kept thinking what a wonderful vehicle it is to expose the atrocities of slavery in the Caribbean, and how with bravery, sacrifice, pride and determination, the slaves eventually were triumphant in bringing an end to this evil practice.

The beautifully vivid imagery of the lush fruit-tree-laden landscape, with the warm glowing sunset as a backdrop, took me back to my days in the more laid-back Jamaican lifestyle, and left me yearning. For others, this setting is an enticing invitation to have a first-hand experience of Jamaica's natural beauty and all of its spoils. I shared in all the excitement, humor, fears, sorrows, joys, losses and achievements of this colorful family, and when the last chapter came to an end I was reluctant to be severed from a world I wanted to continue wrapping myself in. I'm filled and still want more!"

- JC LODGE, RECORDING ARTIST / SONG WRITER, UK

"Like all writers of original and cultural genius, Ms. Jennings awakens our minds and soul in her story of Jamaica, as Bob Marley has with Jamaican reggae music."

- PROFESSOR J.B. "PEANUTS" TAYLOR, M.B.E. J.P. NASSAU, BAHAMAS

$\mathcal{T}$HIS BOOK IS DEDICATED TO MY FATHER Clovis Gladstone Jennings (Mass Pet), whose subtle influence created the kind rebel in my soul, and whose loving spirit continues to nurture and sustain me. May the black butterfly take him on adventures beyond his wildest dreams, and may an enduring peace be with him.

Norma Jennings

Contents

chapter 1

The Departure

JAMAICA IS CALLING ME AGAIN!

Beloved Jamaica, the island of my birth, where brilliant sunshine and glistening white-sand beaches demand reverence; and where the fruit is sweet and abundant. Exotic Jamaica, the island of my muse, where fowl feathers are fervently plucked so there is fresh poultry on the table; where I'm chastised for chatting in Patois (the local dialect) and not the Queen's English; and where I'm lulled to sleep by loud pelts of rain on a tin roof. Profound Jamaica is where I encountered joy, abandon, intrigue and adventure; where I gripped an old midwife's hand and pushed my firstborn through my loins; where the people are strong, defiant and accomplished; and where my loved ones flourished and perished. And Jamaica, my island of rare dismay, is where grace and conflict always compete for regard, and where ancestral struggles and modern-day politics challenge any psyche.

Twickenham in Jamaica is also calling me again!

Rich-and-conflicting Twickenham, where I galloped through tall grass, flirted with the supernatural, communed with harrowing and notorious ancestors, embraced my uniqueness, and learned that heritage influences character.

Childhood in Jamaica is calling me again! I pause, I listen, and this time I surrender.

Four young attendants lowered a small mahogany coffin into the grave on crude, calico-cotton belts. They sweated profusely and muttered to each other in Patois. Then everyone scooped up dirt and threw a handful into the grave out of respect for "poor Miss Jenny," my mother's friend. The weeping and wailing intensified into horrifying screams — and one emotionally distressed woman yelled at the top of her lungs, "Mamma gone, Lord, Mamma gone!"

Then she leaped feet first into the grave. The weary grave attendants sighed because their next task would be to pull Miss Lucy, who was over 250 pounds, out of the grave. This was one hell of a challenge, as she flailed around, squirming like an animal in pain, shrieking over and over, "Mama gone, aaay, Mama gone."

Miss Lucy was finally hauled out of the grave, totally disheveled, without her hat, every hair on her head standing on end, face all wet with sweat and tears. She had generated much body odor from the grave-jumping drama — and now she wore only one shoe.

This spectacle confronted my mother Miss Birdie and me, as the funeral was our first stop in Portland Cottage, the small town where my grandmother lived. We had traveled slowly for over five miles on unpaved roads from Lionel Town, where our family lived. The old jalopy had pulled up to a gathering of about 30 people, all dressed in their Sunday best. They were rocking and singing a most mournful hymn, "Abide with Me." It was the typical Jamaican funeral, with loud singing and several women bawling at the top of their lungs. One woman wailed so hysterically she fell to the ground, while others tried to comfort her and get her back on her feet. The country preacher raised his hand and hollered, "And the dead in Christ shall rise up to meet Jesus on that special Day of Judgment!"

I clutched my mother's frock with both hands, burying my face into the cloth on her belly. The singing, rocking and wailing continued for what seemed like an eternity. Miss Birdie's belly pulsated under her frock as she belted out hymn after hymn with that massive voice of hers. I remember thinking she should be singing on the stage in an opera. "Oh, how I hope to grow up with a voice like hers," I thought to myself. These thoughts diverted my attention and comforted me, as the weeping and wailing rose to a feverish pitch. I peeked out from my hiding place to see the country preacher raise his trembling arms. He bellowed, "Ashes to ashes, and dust to dust, in Jesus' name, amen and amen!"

As others in the congregation tried to console the hefty woman just fished from the grave, more dreary and mournful hymn singing accompanied dirt shoveling, until a neat mound formed on top of the grave. A large, crude cross was stuck on top of the mound to memorialize "poor Miss Jenny," as the crowd walked away from the grave site, glancing back in sorrow. I looked back at the wooden cross, perched against a beautiful orange-and-yellow Caribbean sunset. It was a relief to be looking back at this spectacle.

As we hurried toward Mass Harry's old car, the mosquitoes began to sing around us and eagerly bite our flesh. Miss Birdie picked me up and plopped me into the car, after several stops to moan about Miss Jenny, what a hard life she had, and how she's gone to her maker in the sky.

We finally headed to my grandmother's house at her estate called Twickenham, with seven passengers instead of three. And at least five others from the funeral chased behind us, yelling, "Mass Harry, beg you a drive just ... down to Main Street."

Mass Harry smashed the accelerator and left the funeral throng in the dust. We headed back through

the town of Portland Cottage at 4:55 p.m. What a
beautiful Sunday afternoon, I thought, now feeling
less traumatized by the dreadful graveyard scene
we'd left behind. Then Mass Harry slowed the
vehicle to a gentle chug.

It was August 1957. As the sun warmly caressed
the old jalopy, a gentle breeze kissed the trees
with a playful promise that made my skin tingle,
and the pink satin ribbon in my hair flap against
my ear with glee. To the right, a countrywoman
headed home with a large pail of water on her head.
Her skin was black as coal, and two thick, short
braids stuck out from under an old yellow scarf
tied roughly around her sweaty head. Her full skirt
swung from side to side as she strode along the
side of the dirt road. I turned around with childish
curiosity and saw that her belly was plump.

"Why is that lady's belly so big, Mama?" I asked.

"She has a baby in her belly, my child," Miss
Birdie lamented.

"How can she carry a full pail of water on her head
and a baby in her belly at the same time, Mama?"

"Ah, my daughter, life can be very tough for some
of these country women," sighed my mother. "Not
only do they have to carry water from the wells for
miles on their heads, but when they get home, they
also have a bunch of hungry bellies to feed."

I looked up at Miss Birdie. "What you mean by
hungry bellies, Mama?"

"Some of these country women have six to 12 children at home to feed, and a man who wants to be fed in more ways than one. When you grow up, you will learn that a woman's work is never done."

We were headed down a winding dirt road toward my grandmother's house at her estate, Twickenham. I was in the front seat of the old car, bouncing up and down as the rocks played havoc on the old tires. In the backseat was the funeral throng, heads and arms hanging out the car window, jabbering away in Patois.

At the wheel, Mass Harry looked far older than his years. His skin was brown and leathery from years of hard work in the blazing Jamaican sun, and his eyes were red and weary. I sat next to my mother, Miss Birdie. She was dressed in black, her brown hair pulled back and neatly coifed under a lovely lavender straw hat.

"Mass Harry, when are we going to reach Sedith's house?"

"Soon," he said. "It's just up the road. Sedith is going to be glad to see you!"

I looked up at Miss Birdie. "Mama, why do they call my grandmother Sedith?"

This time, Mass Harry answered, glancing sideways at me with a big grin.

"Everybody in the village calls your grandmother Sedith. Sedith is the short version of Miss Edith. We all love the old lady. She feeds many of our children and gives of us work at Twickenham during hard times. She is like an angel from heaven."

Fifteen minutes later, we pulled up in front of a small, red-roofed cottage that was invitingly framed with a charming veranda. I looked up curiously at the old wooden emblem that said "Twickenham." As Miss Birdie got out of the car and opened the double-iron gates, I saw two inviting bamboo-and-cane rocking chairs on the veranda, moving slowly to and fro in the warm Caribbean breeze.

We drove slowly through Twickenham's gates, and there she was — a simply dressed, slim, elegant older woman. She stood proudly, a natural beauty, with wavy, salt-and-pepper hair pulled back into a long-and-ample braid. Her locks framed the most beautifully scrubbed almond-colored face I'd ever seen. She was definitely of an exotic ethnic mix. I didn't know it then, but that old woman was about to become a defining presence in my life.

"Where have you been all this time? I was worried about the two of you!" declared Sedith.

"It was a long and rough ride," Miss Birdie said. "I think Mass Harry picked the biggest rocks to ride over. At times I thought my belly would leave my body; but we got here in one piece, thank God!"

"We were running late, Sedith," Mass Harry explained, "so I took them straight to Miss Jenny's funeral. Miss Birdie didn't want to miss saying her goodbyes."

This was my first memory of my grandmother Sedith and the estate called Twickenham. Miss Birdie said that we were together many times before, when I was only a baby. After a few minutes of chatter about how Miss Jenny just up and died, and how Sedith went to the church service but not to the gravesite because, "My nerves just couldn't take the bawling and wailing today," we waved goodbye to Mass Harry. I watched with amusement as the old car made its way down the rocky-dirt road, through bushes and around trees, backseat passengers' heads bumping up and down like country bumpkins in a donkey cart.

Sedith's maid Cookie had dinner waiting, and we sat down around the ornate antique mahogany dining table to a meal of rice and peas, stewed beef, and the sweetest lemonade made of brown sugar, fresh lime juice and water. My sister Dahlia did not attend the funeral. She sat across from me at the dinner table, and as I ate and swung my feet up and down under Sedith's linen tablecloth, she smiled and winked at me.

Dahlia had lived with Sedith for several years. I vaguely remembered meeting her earlier. I later learned that she was my father's child from his first marriage. She was 12 years old with a beautiful slender frame, and her long, thick black hair was parted down the middle and braided in two. She was a charming girl, smart and "quite the athlete," according to Sedith. I was immediately drawn to her kind, innocent, unassuming face and knew right then that she would be a lifelong partner, sister and friend.

After dinner and some more chatter, Miss Birdie stood up from the table and declared, "I left my handkerchief at the funeral yard, and I'm going to search for it. I'll be back in just a few minutes."

But I did not see Miss Birdie for four long years after that departure. In all her innocence, this was my mother's way of saying goodbye because, she later told me, she didn't want to see me cry. Miss Birdie left the island to join my father, Mass Pet, in England. My father worked as an engineer throughout Europe, and England would be his home base for the next four years.

Living with Sedith was a privilege by Portland Cottage's standards. She was the major landowner of the area, a prominent member of the local Adventist church, and the village's matriarch. Indeed, she was a woman with the presence of a fallen queen. Sedith's pride, pomp and stiff upper lip reflected her role as the village's most influential woman. The stiff upper lip was a result of her British upbringing, which included strong discipline and the attitude of "never let them see you sweat." Elegance, kindness and class — Sedith was blessed with these remarkable qualities.

NORMA JENNINGS

chapter 2

Twickenham:
The Playground

*M*Y GRANDMOTHER SEDITH WAS THE
heir to Twickenham, an old sugarcane plantation
passed down through the generations by Andrew
Reid. Reid was a plantation owner of Scottish
descent. A widow, the mother of four children, and
the owner of 218 acres of land, Sedith was a force
to be reckoned with in the small town of Portland
Cottage where Twickenham is located. She was
well respected, actively involved in the community,
and held strong religious beliefs. I spent four of my
formative years with the old lady, and she helped
mold me into the woman I was to become.

After Miss Birdie left to retrieve her handkerchief
and did not return, I sat on an old wooden bench in
Sedith's dining room and cried for hours. The old
lady's efforts to comfort me were fruitless, and now

I was the one weeping for my mother.

The abandonment I felt was overwhelming. My sister Dahlia eventually got me to stop crying. Every morning before leaving for school, her hugs and hot mugs of Milo comforted the little girl who felt like a motherless child. Every day I waited under a large Bombay mango tree at Twickenham's gate for Dahlia to come home. Sounds of children playing, fighting and laughing as they headed home conjured up my anticipation and excitement that Dahlia was on her way.

Evenings with Dahlia were filled with mischief and lots of antics. I would pinch her, giggle and wait impatiently as she did homework. Then we would play hopscotch, have spirited feather pillow fights, and gallop like wild horses through Twickenham until dusk.

One afternoon before Dahlia got home from school, I gathered the courage to explore Twickenham alone. With bare feet, I pranced playfully through a sea of tall, mature grass that all but engulfed my slender, five-year-old frame. In full motion, I stretched my arms outward and as my fingers fleetingly caressed soft grass plumes, the warm Caribbean breeze cleared a golden path before me.

A guava tree ahead bent gracefully with ripe fruit begging to be picked, as a hummingbird fluttered merrily from fruit to fruit, relishing each aroma and flavor. Oh how I wished I could fly and savor, just like that fortuitous little creature.

And look at that display of purple "coolie plums" on the tree unveiling to my right. If my belly wasn't protruding with brown-stewed chicken and rice and peas from my grandmother's kitchen, this smorgasbord of fresh tropical fruit would certainly be at my mercy. But alas, my eyes were bigger than my bowel.

After breezing by an array of other trees heavily laden with fruit, I finally beheld the ultimate prize … a Bombay mango tree pleading for attention. It was a compelling sight; chock-full of mangoes ripened by the stunning Caribbean sun that now dozed in a westerly cradle, boasting hues of yellow, orange and purple.

Yearning for dessert, I squatted, and then leapt and grabbed a branch, pulled myself up onto the trunk of the tree, and began my greedy climb. I'm salivating while advancing toward the succulent reward that awaited me … a perfectly ripe, bright-yellow mango with an orange glow on one side, just like this evening's sunset. My lips smacked with anticipation … it was a pearl in an ocean of fresh jewels. My left foot stumbled on a brittle tree branch. It was a close call. I anxiously grabbed a lush green branch above to save myself from obvious mutilation waiting below. I contained myself and continued the journey upward.

Then ah, my right hand finally caressed the gem that had been provoking my pallet. I perched myself contentedly on a sturdy branch and sunk my teeth into that luscious feast. Then I buried my face into pure ecstasy and slurped for what felt like nirvana, coming up for air and ravenous chewing. Now my face was covered in an orange glow. Anything better than this must be the heaven that Parson Mitchell preaches about in church on Saturdays.

Bliss is crudely interrupted by a high-pitched shriek from Cookie, my grandmother's maid.

"Miss Olivia, come down from that tree right now. Your grandmother wants you in the house and in the bathtub this very minute!"

I scampered down the tree of my delight and sprinted home, knowing for sure that I would be back for more first thing tomorrow morning.

Church on Saturday was an all-day event. We went to morning service, home to a light lunch, and followed Sedith like ducklings to afternoon and evening services — it was all at once entertaining, tedious, comforting and frightening. Parson Mitchell's harangues about brimstone and fire brought visions and nightmares about Judgment Day: "The coming of the Lord on his mighty throne to judge who will go to glory, or burn in the mighty fires of hell."

Cookie saved the day and helped us forget the Parson's tirades by whipping up her best meals after sundown. Dahlia and I eagerly devoured Cookie's sumptuous brown-stewed chicken, steamed fish, rice and peas, ripe plantains and dessert dishes of sweet tropical fruit or moist bread pudding with the "hallelujah" on top, a crown of the pudding plumped with raisins and warm cream.

The old preacher could also be entertaining. One Saturday during one of his spirited sermons, we heard chickens cackling outside of the church window — a hungry mongoose was chasing them. In the middle of Parson Mitchell's shouts, "And the Lord said unto Moses," he turned his head toward the noise and continued, "mongoose into the bush there you know!"

Dahlia and I were now the ones cackling like hens. We covered our mouths, and with eyes bulging, we tried to stop ourselves from rolling on the church floor with fits of laughter. Sedith snarled, "One more sound and the two of you will feel the sting of my belt after Sabbath."

That growl kept us quiet. Now we were unsure what would be worse: the sting of Sedith's belt or the brimstone and fire extolled by the passionate old Adventist preacher.

Sundays at Twickenham were wild and exciting too. We sprinted through the bushes and scuttled up the tropical fruit trees that made Sedith's yard so popular with the neighborhood children. We would gorge our bellies with mangoes, guavas, sweetsops, naseberries and coconuts. By the time Sedith called us in for dinner, our bellies were already protruding with fruit; but her threats of "eat your dinner or you will feel my belt" had us gobbling down more food.

Then we would set off on another gallop through Twickenham to blow off steam and absorb Cookie's cuisine. And the old maid had no qualms about chasing us through bushes and up trees when we refused to heed Sedith's beckoning, armed only with her big, rusty soupspoon.

Cookie was the fattest, blackest countrywoman I'd ever seen, with miraculous culinary skills. This evening her curried goat and rice definitely made the soupspoon chases worth the sprint. Besides, we were young and full of energy. As we sped through the tall grass of Twickenham, with warm tropical breezes pounding our faces, we giggled with delight as Cookie muttered breathlessly behind us, "Where them little devils gone? Lord, these rude mulatto pickaninnies going to be the death of me!"

Our parents were still in England at the time, so my three brothers lived in Kingston with Miss Birdie's mother, our other grandmother everyone called Miss Vie. Clinton was the youngest and most mischievous of the gang. He arrived at Twickenham for holidays during my first summer with Sedith. He was a handsome boy, with smooth olive skin, huge brown eyes and curly brown hair. And his stinging punches and running speed had me getting my fists and sprint in gear so I could survive his visit.

My brother's first summer at Twickenham was packed with fun, excitement, adventure, Sedith's belt, and lots of Cookie's rusty soupspoon-wielding chases. By week two, he would learn the lay of the land. We were playing outside Twickenham's gates when a donkey cart came roaring by at full speed, captained by Mass Joe. Clinton exclaimed, "Let's go have some fun, Sis. Follow me!"

We raced barefoot behind the donkey cart, jumped on board next to the old man, right on our bony behinds. Powered by two huge donkeys, there we went, galloping down Portland Cottage road bumping and rocking, our bodies slamming on the cart's wooden floor. Clinton laughed, "We'll get our backsides belted after this, Sis, but let's worry about that later."

Then he glanced up and yelled, "What a way these donkeys can gallop! Mass Joe, what have you been feeding these donkeys? They gallop like racehorses!"

Mass Joe responded with a thunderous and boastful, "Yaaaaaaaaa!" as the donkeys sprinted faster and faster, much to our delight.

Minutes later, the tropical foliage changed to beautiful views of sea grapes and almond trees. The sea smell greeted us, and soon we pulled up to a beautiful white-sand beach in front of a vast, inviting, turquoise Caribbean Sea. At last, we were at Jackson's Bay! We jumped out of the cart, dove into the crystal-clear, shallow water, and spent the rest of the day catching fish or searching for alligators in the swamp.

The unspoiled beaches of Jackson's Bay framed the southern border of Twickenham. The whole day could pass on that secluded beach with only an occasional fisherman in his colorful canoe passing by in the distance. I looked up at one of Twickenham's mountains and imagined the incredible scenery from there. Clinton jolted me back to reality, making up wild stories to tell Sedith when we got home. We prayed for protection from the sting of her belt. "Let's tell her we were kidnapped by wooden-leg Charlie," he said.

"No, no, let's say we got lost in the bushes, chased by a wild boar, and it took all day for us to find our way home!"

But as Mass Joe's donkey cart roared closer to home, we sighed and resigned ourselves to the whipping. No stories would save us. We would have been missing for six hours. Ah, but what great fun we had!

We had barely recovered from the excitement and joy of our donkey-driven adventure, when one week later we were faced with a creepy and gut-wrenching experience. On a balmy Sunday afternoon Clinton and I pranced through

Twickenham, dodging trees, with big, old cotton caps pulled over our brows and catapults hanging from our back pockets in case some poor, unfortunate and edible tropical bird flew by. We stopped dead in our tracks and peeked from behind some bushes to behold a country funeral in progress next door.

As we inched our way behind old Miss Edna's one-room wooden house, we peeked nervously at the gravediggers, sweating like pigs, wielding rusty old iron shovels, drinking white rum and chatting loudly in Patois. One yelled, "No man, dig this side deeper; this is where the head of the coffin will be."

"Pass me another shot of the white rum," the other said.

A few guests in their Sunday best milled around, talking about how Miss Edna's daughter dropped dead in England, and how the body had to be flown back to Jamaica for burial in the family's yard. One woman lamented how scary it was that Jamaicans were dropping dead from hard work in England and America, and their bodies were sent home and put to rest.

Our mouths flew open as a gravedigger let out an ear-piercing yell, "Oh Lord!"

He rose from the grave with a clammy, dripping skull in hand. Miss Edna bolted toward her nearby house screaming, "Oh God, that is my son!"

In seconds, she was racing frantically back to the grave, dragging an old white sheet. With anguish in her eyes, she grabbed the skull and what looked like some old bones, hurriedly wrapped them in the sheet, and ran back into her house screaming, "My son! They dug up my son!"

With lightening speed and kicking up dust, we left that scene, fleeing through the woods back to Sedith's house. Our hearts racing, jumping over bushes, ducking tree branches in our fastest ever barefoot marathon, I grabbed the back of Clinton's shirt to keep up with him. He shucked it off into my hands and sped ahead like a bullet. It was about to get worse. We put our brakes on to avoid crashing into Cookie who was suddenly in front of us, staring us down, wide-eyed, and armed with the big, rusty soupspoon. She yelled, "Your grandmother wants you in the house for dinner right now!"

We gingerly approached Sedith's dining room, trembling and breathing heavily. As we sat down around the big mahogany dining table, Sedith smiled sadistically and announced, "It's calf's liver, rice and peas, and fried plantains for dinner. Start licking your lips because it is delicious!"

After what we had just witnessed in Miss Edna's yard, we clutched our throats, gagging and coughing at the sight of liver on our plates. Like trapped animals, we gobbled down the food, trying to hide our disgust, and to avoid the infamous belt. Sedith stared at us with playful curiosity, going "mmmmm!" as if to taunt us.

Without a doubt, the sweet tropical flavors of Cookie's cuisine helped us keep dinner down in our nervous bellies. That evening, the wild adventure through Twickenham left us exhausted. As we flopped down into some tall grass, Clinton exclaimed, "My God, I will not eat liver again 'till the day I die!"

War and defiance — that's what Clinton waged with Sedith about what he called the Saturday "all-day church business." He woke early, climbed up one of the naseberry trees, and stared down as Sedith waved the belt, threatening and pleading with him to come down and get dressed. Dahlia and I got ready as usual for "the all-day church business." We were smart. We knew that when Clinton returned to Kingston after summer holidays, we would be at Sedith's mercy. Sedith, now exhausted, gave up, and left for church with her two granddaughters close behind in their Sunday dresses and crinolines. We glanced back grudgingly at Clinton in the tree, sticking out his tongue at us as if to say "suckers!" We knew he would be catapulting birds, roaming the bushes, and stuffing his gut with fresh fruit. And damn it, we were preparing to endure more of Parson Mitchell's passionate brimstone and fire sermons.

The next summer, we were shipped off to our Cousin Todd's home. Cousin Todd was the "Busha" of a tropical fruit and cattle farm in St. Thomas,

Jamaica. We were put on a big, old country bus, and the driver was clearly instructed to let us off at the 36th milepost. Talk about excitement. As the bus careened around corners, leaning almost on two wheels over precipices, we would close our eyes and wince with fear. My belly ached with dread that the huge crocus bags of food, clothes and other wares roped tightly on top of the bus would send us careening into a deep ravine. Later, with brakes screeching followed by a loud blast of the horn, the bus driver yelled, "OK, children, this is Prospect Beach, and it is where you get off. I'll wait 'till your family comes out to get you."

We looked up, and there it was on a hill across the beach — Prospect Estate, our latest summer home of fun and adventure. Sedith had told us that the estate had six bedrooms, a vast veranda, and an enchanting history. We rushed uphill just as Cousin Todd came out of the house to greet us. Clinton and I looked back and waved, as the old bus blasted its horn and slowly accelerated into the sunset, leaning precariously to one side. Cousin Todd's warm welcome made us feel right at home. We jumped up and down, clutching our bags with excitement and laughing with rollicking anticipation.

We climbed trees, drove tractors, milked cows, and floated fearlessly in the ocean on a huge inner tube. Most of us could barely swim, but we were bold. Dinners were tasty island dishes lovingly cooked by the maids. Desserts of delicious mango halves filled with rum-and-raisin ice cream kept us humble. In the mornings, we awoke to sounds of the maids' chatter. We would peek through the windows to see them boiling fresh cow's milk in massive-and-shiny tin buckets on crackling wood fires. We ran out the door and rallied for the green light to skim fresh cream from the top of each bucket with a big wooden spoon and savor the fresh, warm taste. Then we were called inside for breakfast of brown-stewed kidneys and boiled green bananas, fresh eggs and ham, ackee and salt fish, dumplings, fried plantains and cassava cakes.

Revelry and tomfoolery summed up our evenings at Prospect. We had pillow fights, pelted each other with ice cubes, and yelled with victory after winning a cutthroat game of dominoes. One night, we heard what sounded like footsteps outside and a dog barking. Cousin Todd's son Andrew grabbed a shotgun and fired one round through the wooden jalousie window. After that, our nights were much quieter. Cousin Todd started sleeping at home instead of at his girlfriend's house to ensure we did no damage to ourselves or to the unfortunate person who may have dodged the bullets fired outside the night before.

One sunny day, Clinton ventured up the biggest mango tree at Prospect Estate to pick and throw ripe mangoes to me on the ground. We planned

a belly-gorging mango feast. I heard the crack
of branches snapping — and as I looked up in a
panic, Clinton was hunched over in a ball, falling
to the ground in somersaults. My outstretched arms
reached out for him. He crashed into me with a
thud! We both fell violently to the ground. With
arms and knees battered and bruised from the tree's
protruding roots, I looked frightfully at my brother
and grabbed onto him. Thank God he was alive! We
knew then that I had saved him from certain death
or physical impairment.

After that, Dahlia and I returned to Twickenham
for school and more of the "all-day church
business." But by next summer, Clinton was back
to kick up more dust and create yet more mischief.
We were now curious about the supernatural. We
wanted to know more about Obeah, Jamaican
voodoo, and to go "duppy" (ghost) hunting.
If Sedith knew what we were planning, she
would certainly kill us. She was a church-going
spiritualist, who thought such "foolishness" was
just like "playing with the devil."

Mystery and the unknown jostled for our
attention. We were about to experience some
voodoo, whether Sedith liked it or not. We heard
from Dulce, a schoolmate who lived in a thatch
house nearby, that the local Obeah man was
about to "raise the dead" at the cemetery behind
Portland Cottage's Episcopal Church. Clinton

and I hid eagerly behind bushes within earshot of the cemetery and waited anxiously. In a nervous whisper, I begged him not to back his shirt off into my hands, if we had to perform a sprint away from the voodoo site; but Clinton grinned mischievously and exclaimed, "Sis, if you can't lead the sprint, then you will be left in the dust."

What the hell, I decided I'd wait for the Obeah man to arrive anyway and deal with the sprint later on.

Mass Boothe, the Obeah man, arrived in full array — with big, crusty bare feet sticking out of pants that looked like they had been hemmed in a flood. A big, floppy white gown hung indelicately over his pants. With huge, red, protruding eyes, his face was wrinkled and haggard. The Obeah man looked like he had just had a fight with the devil, and he had three women in tow dressed in old white gowns, their heads wrapped in matching cloth. Mass Boothe's followers resembled the devil's angels.

By now it was dusk, and the Obeah workers started prancing around a grave with fearless animation. Mass Boothe began chanting several times in unknown tongues, "Asta la dooche, ummmmm, ummmmmm, talliwaah, ju, ju."

I glanced behind, and Clinton's eyes were bulging out of their sockets. Then I spun around and saw what looked like thin, white smoke ascending slowly from the grave being disturbed by the Obeah man. Ah, what's a girl to do but take off in the opposite direction, sprinting through brush, jumping over thorny bushes, viewing the back of Clinton's shirt flapping in the wind way ahead? I thought, "Sedith warned us against having anything to do with the local Obeah man. She said he was like the devil — but no, we didn't listen. We had to see it for ourselves."

This time, Cookie wasn't waiting to ambush us with the soupspoon. We holed up in the corner of one of our bedrooms, shaking like scared animals, and Sedith kept asking with grandmotherly concern, "What's wrong with you two? You look like you've seen a ghost."

We made her no wiser, but that night I had Clinton swear we would leave the Obeah men of Portland Cottage alone!

The next day Sedith was jolly. She announced that she was taking us on a tour of Twickenham. As she walked the property, we were right next to her in a quick stride, and she pointed to a large concrete slab.

"That is the foundation of the old great house where the Scotsman Ian Reid lived with his concubines. Over there is Puss Gully where the slaves hid before bolting for the hills."

Sedith bent down, dug her fingers into the dirt, and announced, "These are pieces of crockery from Ian Reid's stash of fine china that he brought to Jamaica from far-off lands."

We looked around in every direction, taking in

the scenery. Twickenham was taking on different dimensions. It was no longer merely Sedith's vast backyard.

"Children," she said, "you will soon hear things about your 'playground' Twickenham that will make your hair stand on end! But this is your heritage, so when the time comes you must listen, and you must listen well."

Norma Jennings

chapter 3

Sedith:
The Storyteller

*R*ESISTANCE. LOUD BLASTS FROM AN
African horn. Escape and savage clashes for
deliverance. We were mere children, but we were
about to experience it all — straight from the lips of
a family legend.

One hot summer night, Sedith sat us down on the
veranda, positioned herself contentedly on one of
the old cane rocking chairs, and announced, "Me
children, I'm about to give you a history lesson that
you'll never forget. The stories I'm sharing tonight
will give clear pictures of our family's past, and
I'm hoping that they will mold you into the adults
you will become. If you know where you're coming
from, you'll know where you're headed in life —
never forget that. The history of our little island
called Jamaica is very rich. It is your heritage; but

believe me, our family history is stronger than you can imagine. So gather round and listen good, me grandchildren."

Sedith did this so well. She spoke the Queen's English when she was serious, yet broke out into Patois during moments of mischief and admonishing. It was an endearing verbal dance in her quest to teach us proper British standards, yet taunt us by communing with the African ancestors while talking Patois.

We sat and squirmed in for space close to Sedith, pushing and shoving each other and complaining. I plopped down into the rocking chair next to hers, elbowing Clinton out of that seat. She had my undivided attention.

Sedith glanced at us, one by one, *"You remember teacher Williams telling you that the Arawak Indians provided Christopher Columbus and his men with provisions to keep them alive after their ships ran ashore in Jamaica in 1492? What a joke; the Indians were here first, yet Columbus "discovered" Jamaica. These poor Indians were repaid with death and destruction by the mid-1600s,"* lamented Sedith. *"Not only were they brutalized and forced to be slaves, many were also shipped off to Spain to serve other masters.*

While this cruelty was going on, the Spanish planters made a decision that would shape the future of Jamaica. They needed more cheap labor to work the plantations, so according to the history books, slaves were brought in from many West African nations such as the Ashanti, Fanti, Akim and other tribes.

Although these slaves were well-known for being rebellious and stubborn, the Spanish planters liked buying them because they were hard-working, strong Mandingo types. These groups of slaves were later called Kromantis, and they were sold to the planters at a very high price. In fact, slave traders claimed that their goods were Kromantis whether they were or not. They made more money this way. The poor slaves were labeled as barbarians to be controlled by brute force.

But many of the Kromantis shipped to Jamaica had already been through strenuous guerrilla warfare training and seasoning in West Africa. Later, the Spanish and English would live to regret their decision to bring these proud rebels into Jamaica, because slave rebellions made their lives on the plantations a living hell.

To the planters, bringing slaves in from different African tribes would fit nicely into the plantation strategy of "divide and rule." The Africans spoke different languages and brought with them diverse cultural rituals. One of these was the voodoo ritual called Obeah that you children are so curious about." Clinton attempted to open his mouth about our bout with the Obeah man. A kick on the shin from me shut him up.

Sedith continued, *"The planters were hoping that
tribal differences would continue on the plantations,
and that this would make their ability to remain in
control much easier.*

*But after they survived the horrible and
sometimes deadly voyage through the Middle
Passage from Africa to the West Indies, the slaves
were further reduced to the cruel and barbaric
sting of the planters' whips. This only made them
stronger and more determined. They came together
and formed new bonds against slavery. Without
a doubt, Kromantis, who later became known as
Maroons, led most of the slave uprisings on our
island in the 17th and 18th centuries.*

*Hundreds of Maroons gradually and successfully
fled the plantations and formed rebel groups. They
were proud and disciplined. And they wreaked
havoc against the planters, who cringed with fear
as these rebels returned with a vengeance to the
plantations on which they were brutalized. The
Maroons set up communities of their own in the
rugged hills and rainforests of Jamaica known
as Nanny Town, Cockpit Country, Accompong,
Guys Town, Cornwall Barracks and Charles Town.
And they also had settlements close to us here at
Twickenham.*

*During these years, the Maroons also got
together with the few Arawak Indians who had
escaped from the Spanish. The Indians provided*

their African friends with lessons in ecology and agriculture. They taught them how to use plants to make medicines and how to survive in the Jamaican bushes. All of this, plus knowledge about the island's terrain, turned the Maroons into skillful warriors. There were stories of Indians fighting side-by-side with Maroons against the planters.

But the history books also tell us that there were problems between Arawaks and Maroons. Maroon rebels were known to capture Arawak Indian women. These women later taught the Africans arts and crafts, basket weaving and pottery. But the poor Arawak Indians were soon totally wiped out.

To make matters worse, the British arrived in Jamaica in the mid-1600s during a time when wars and conflicts between Spain and Britain for West Indian territories were rampant. The British envied what they thought was the success the Spanish had already been enjoying in the Caribbean. So they got into the action of capturing our islands in order to fatten their own pockets. During this time, the waters of the Caribbean were infested with pirates sent to sea by European governments to plunder and pillage their way into Jamaica and other islands nearby — my grandchildren, that is how pirates like Captain Morgan, who is now buried at Port Royal, ended up in Jamaica.

But things got even worse, depending on how you look at it. When the British invaded Jamaica, they slaughtered the Spanish by the hundreds. Those who survived abandoned their plantations and fled to Cuba, the Dominican Republic, and other Spanish-speaking Caribbean islands. This was a great opportunity for the slaves remaining on the Spanish plantations to take to the hills in droves and join the communities of free Maroons.

The British royally arrived in Jamaica without knowing what waited for them in the hills of Cockpit Country, Nanny Town, Accompong, and other hidden Maroon communities. By then, the Afro-Jamaican Maroons were strong, proud and relentless, and they forcefully rejected any form of control and bruteforce against black people.

The British invasion brought hundreds of Englishmen and some Welsh, Irish and Scotsmen who had failed to succeed in their homelands as farmers. They saw Jamaica and other islands as quick routes to wealth.

Soon after their arrival, sugar became the "white gold" of the islands. However, making sugar required a lot of human labor. Africans were again stolen from their homeland to work as slaves and to transform our Jamaica into one of the most profitable colonies now owned by the British.

Many Africans actually died, and their bodies were dumped overboard during the devastating journey to the West Indies. Due to this high death rate, there was a constant demand to replace slave *labor. And those Africans unfortunate enough to survive the voyage were about to receive a brutal introduction to what was waiting for them on the plantations here.*

Brutally long hours of labor daily were common for the slaves and during the indoctrination period they were given very little food. To add to the misery, the whip cracked frequently to force more hard work and to provide a constant reminder of who was the master. Many slaves did not survive this. And those who did not die from exhaustion died because they were not able to adjust to the stresses of this harsh lifestyle.

Despite these hardships, the slaves who survived plantation life developed their own ways to resist the system and continued to reject the concept of black inferiority. Passive resistance or all-out guerrilla warfare occurred daily, and the more resistance from the slaves, the more afraid the planters became. The result was more beatings and a vicious cycle of uprisings and fear. Despite this, very few days went by on this little island without strong defiance and revolts.

The slaves who survived used a number of tactics to get by. They "played fool to catch wise" just like you children do when you don't want to do your chores. The planters viewed this as "these negroes are so dumb," but to the slaves this ploy meant, "let's make the master think we're stupid." Then there was refusal to work or working very slowly, which was labeled by the Brits as "lazy negroes." And let's not forget trickery to confuse the master, viewed by the planters as "these negroes are liars." The planters were now experiencing willful acts of passive resistance by blacks against slavery.

But the constant violent rebellion did the most damage and made its mark on Jamaica's plantations. So many slaves had been brought into the island that by the mid-to-late 1700s, African people outnumbered plantation whites by nine-to-one. The planters were truly feeling what it was like to be fearful and threatened as Maroon attacks and slave rebellions became even more brutal and relentless. As their fears rose, so did their brutality; their only way of attempting to stay in control.

Despite this, there were daily escapes from the plantations as the Maroon communities grew, and house slaves secretly provided them with information from conversations they overheard at the massa's dinner table. That information played a big role in the success of frequent and bloody Maroon raids.

For close to 85 years, Maroon raids never ceased, and the planters, fearful and overwhelmed, appealed to Britain for military assistance. For years, their attempts to negotiate with the Maroons were rejected and met with more fury. The Maroon mentality said, "There will be no peace as *long as you are brutalizing our brothers on your plantations."*

These threats got so intense the planters did not know whom to trust. Some losses that resembled death from diseases or natural causes were actually due to other reasons such as suspected food poisoning. As a result, the planters needed to be good to their cooks or they could end up dead.

The planters did get help from the British, but when they sent troops to Jamaica, they greatly misjudged the strength, cunning and resolve of the black rebels from the mountains. The Maroons' total understanding of the local terrain was superior, and their African and Arawak military training prepared them to take on any enemy attempting to attack them. They had become brilliant masters of disguise and hit-and-run guerrilla strategies, and the British army had never experienced anything similar. By the time the Brits would advance on them, all stiff in uniform and armed with bayonets, the Maroons had already sent out spies who reported precise information on troop size, weapons and location. They were able to fully disguise themselves with local plants, and even covered up the scent of their bodies so that no one could identify their locations.

Maroons lay in wait close to the British troops, and when they unleashed their ferocious assault, all the British troops saw was what looked like trees and plants attacking them.

Then sudden destruction hit, as machetes chopped off heads from what the Brits thought was a bush in the forest, and then the Maroons would quickly vanish. The cunning Maroons had successfully combined traditional African guerrilla warfare with Arawak Indian fighting techniques, and they were now unbeatable. Another amazing fact is that the Maroons knew how to build smokeless fires, which helped keep their whereabouts a secret. Did you know that Jamaica's authentic hot-and-spicy jerk cuisine that is cooked on hot coals underground, came to us from the smokeless fire of Maroon cooking?"

We listened intently. We were impressed with her wealth of knowledge. We had no idea that Cookie's delicious jerk chicken came from the Maroons. Sedith thoughtfully continued.

"The Maroons also completely confused and terrified the British soldiers by communicating using bird sounds, drums and the abeng horn. The Maroons were also helped by the snakes and malaria-carrying mosquitoes that had their share of the British soldiers, who had much lower resistance to tropical illnesses.

Throughout this period of slaughter and confusion, sounds of the abeng horn and "put-um, put-um" chants of the Afro-Jamaican drums motivated more slaves to escape and join free and ferocious Maroon communities. As escaped slaves joined them, the Maroons put them through rapid training in warfare.

The British troops suffered severe losses, and there were constant requests for replacements; but soldiers in Britain dreaded assignments to fight the black rebels in Jamaica. Most viewed this as a death sentence. Word got around that fighting with bayonets was far inferior to Maroon tactics in the rugged terrain of our little island. Bayonets had to be reloaded after each shot, and any attempt to do this could be fatal as Maroons converged and chopped the soldiers to pieces.

"Oh shit!" yelled Clinton, face red with excitement.

"Calm down boy, before I have to get me belt and do a number on you behind," Sedith threatened. We were again amused by her ability to go in and out of Patois, depending on whether she was threatening or storytelling. This verbal dance with the British and African ancestors really helped keep us captivated. Sedith pressed on.

"In the end, the British troops were beaten during every attack. And the Maroons managed to do this with minimum risk to their own men. They had won, both morally and on the battlefield. They had worn the planters down and had hit them where it hurt most — in the pocket and on the battlefield. After all attempts by the British to rid our island of free-black communities had failed, and at a very

bloody cost, it became apparent they could only save the colony of Jamaica by negotiating peace with the Maroons."

And Sedith wrapped it up by saying, *"To this day, my grandchildren, Jamaicans stand-up for themselves as they cope with life's problems. Slavery is of no importance to our people, but defiance against cruel and unfair treatment is a part of our character."*

chapter 4

Twickenham: The Beginning

CRUELTY, PASSION, ADVENTURE AND greed ... from her lips to our ears. Sedith's next storytelling session truly challenged our existence.

On a warm Friday evening, Cookie called us down from the fruit trees of Twickenham. "You grandmother want you inside the house right now! Don't make me have to chase after you today. I'm too tired, and I may lose me temper real fast."

Sitting in her favorite chair on the veranda, Sedith yelled, "Cookie, bring a dozen guavas for the children. They will be sitting here with me for a long time this evening, and they'll need comfort food." She stared off into the distance, and I thought, "Let the story begin ..."

"This evening we going to learn about your great, great, great, even more infamous grandfather named Ian Reid who migrated to Jamaica in the late 1700s."

We rushed for front seats again. We knew that Sedith's stories were about to get really personal, but we weren't expecting juicy. And so her story began:

"According to my grandmother and your great grandmother, Ian Reid was born and raised in Stobhill, a small town in Scotland near Glasgow. His parents were from modest means. He was an average student in high school and after graduation, he went to explore job opportunities in a place I believe she called it Lincoln, England. His father, Robert Reid, worked as overseer on a small farm in Stobhill, and Ian had worked there as a farmhand during the last two summers of high school.

Four weeks after arriving in Lincoln, Ian landed a job as a farmhand on a 50-acre estate on the outskirts of town. The work was grueling, but he made a living. He shared a room on the compound with two co-workers, John Cole and Christopher Thomas. On Friday and Saturday nights, the three could be seen drinking beer and carousing in the local pubs with others from the compound, singing loudly, and challenging each other at spirited games of dominoes and darts.

One warm Saturday night in July, they were at a local pub playing darts, when Ian saw on the other side of the bar Olga, daughter of Ben Murphy, sitting on a barstool. Murphy was the boss and the owner of the farm where Ian worked. Olga wore a short, hot-pink sundress with half of her bosoms bulging at the neckline like two overblown balloons about to explode."

We were shocked by Sedith's unexpected and graphic description of Olga. Dahlia and I put our hands over our mouths to muffle laughter. Clinton's eyes bulged, and his smirk said he didn't know whether to laugh or get excited; but the old lady was on a roll now, so we quieted down and allowed our deeply religious grandmother to enjoy the astonishment on our faces.

She shot us a mischievous grin and teased, "Clinton, pick up you bottom lip from off the veranda floor so I can continue the story." I was again amazed at how quickly she switched from the Queen's English to Patois, depending on whether she was taunting us or telling riveting stories.

She proceeded, savoring the moment. *"Olga's long blond hair was brushed softly on her freckled, fragile shoulders. She sent Ian a sultry, seductive look across the bar. Christopher, who missed nothing, saw Olga's come-hither look. "Blimey, Ian, I think she wants you. Think you have the balls to take that on? I hear she's an alley cat in the boudoir."*

Rising slowly from his chair, glass of dark beer in hand, chest out like a peacock, Ian sighed dramatically. "Watch me and weep, bloke. Just call me 'Tom Cat,' because I'm about to purrrrrr ... meow!"

He strutted over to Olga, whose hungry baby-blue eyes followed him slowly and deliberately across the room. "Olga," he said, "fancy meeting you here. What a pleasure!"

Olga held out her delicate hand to him and said in a sultry, subdued voice, "The pleasure is all mine, bloke. Pull up a chair and let's have a good chat."

Ian gently kissed her hand, slid on the stool facing her, and stared into her blue eyes. They talked and flirted for over two hours. Around midnight, Olga asked him to walk her home. Before they left, Ian went over to John and Christopher, leaned in, and whispered with a mischievous wink, "Don't you blokes even think about going home for the next two hours because the two cats, 'Tom and Alley' are about to take a romp and raise some hell. Not sure where, but we may need the room."

Ian and Olga set out for the farm under the stars, which according to some, were rarely seen in English skies. She snuggled up to him, and he put his arm around her tiny waist. As they approached the sprawling main house, Ian was conjuring sweet words to keep Olga with him and extend the evening, but she skillfully steered him toward the horse barn.

Inside, she closed the door and pushed him down

on a stack of hay. She slowly unbuttoned the front of her sexy sundress to reveal two of the most round and perky breasts Ian had ever seen. "My God, I'm about to be had by Ben Murphy's pride and joy," he thought, succumbing to the warmth of her firm, full breasts pressed on top of his bare, muscular chest. Her sweet breath blew gently against his ear. Her full lips found his. They surrendered to deep, long and passionate kisses. After an eternity, he kneeled over her and began to remove his clothes. She slowly slithered out of her dress and panties, lifted her right leg, and skillfully maneuvered both pants and underwear from his throbbing body with her bare toes. She kissed and licked him passionately as she enveloped his throbbing flesh into hers."

By now, not only were my eyes bulging with disbelief, Dahlia leaned over to me and whispered, "Now you take your bottom lip off the floor, Miss Olivia. We've just had a quick-and-dirty lesson in sex education from one of Parson Mitchell's favorite church sisters."

We glanced over at Clinton, whose lips were now trembling with disbelief as he salivated, slowly chewed on a guava, and tried to compose himself.

Sedith was definitely on a roll and she pressed on. *"After that night of pure ecstasy, Olga and Ian could not stay away from each other. They met at least two nights a week to make passionate love in the barn, in the grass behind the barn, and in his bed after he'd told his roommates to "take a hike for a good two hours." John and Christopher returned grumbling about how the "alley cat" was wearing Ian out. They couldn't wait to "behold the brimstone and fire that would erupt when boss-man Ben Murphy found out that Ian, the farmhand from Scotland, was 'bashing his innocent daughter,' the 'alley cat in disguise.'"*

For three months, Olga and Ian caroused at the local pubs and seized every opportunity to wear each other out in the hay. Ian was completely consumed with her. Their passionate encounters had become the talk of farmhands. Christopher grudgingly asked him, "What are your plans, bloke? Do you continue to let her wear you out, or do you put her out of her misery? Marry her and get on with it, for Christ's sake!"

"I'm madly in love with her," Ian said. "And I'm thinking of asking old man Murphy for her hand in marriage. You think he'll turn his nose up that I'm not good enough for her?"

Christopher looked him dead in the eyes and muttered, teeth clenched, "I think old man Murphy is going to kill you after he's totally mutilated your Scottish backside, that's what I think. If you have any delusions about him turning the farm over to the likes of you because you're in love with his Olga, you can forget it. I hear he's been trying to marry her off to Tom Williams, the son of that wealthy 500-

acre farm owner outside of town. I'm warning you, Ian, these rich Brits stick together. I'd watch my back, if I were you!"

By then it was the beginning of October. The chill and gloom of a long and grey English winter was in the air. The horse barn was now a less-desirable love nest. As Ian pondered his next move, Olga knocked on his bedroom door.

"Ian, I have to talk to you in private. Can you come out for a stroll?"

Ian quickly dressed and went outside to walk hand in hand with her through the woods behind the barn. Fearfully, with tears in her eyes, Olga announced, "I'm pregnant. Daddy is going to kill me!"

Ian stopped in his tracks. He tried to be calm as he absorbed the shock of her words. "Are ... are you sure? When did you find out?"

She calmed down. "I was four weeks late and my friend Martha took me to see Doctor Taylor. He ran the tests. I'm already six weeks gone. What are we going to do?"

Ian looked Olga in the eyes, "How do you think old man Murphy would feel if we were to get married? I love you, Olga. We could raise our child together."

They decided to tell Murphy the following Monday after dinner. Ian planned to stop by the house during tea and crumpets. They would break the news.

But the talk with Olga's father was a disaster. Ben

Murphy went into a violent rage, pointing one of his bayonets directly into Ian's terrified face.

"I do you a favor, give your Scottish backside work and a place to live, and you repay me by bashing and breeding my innocent young daughter? Get your backside off my farm before I blow you to pieces. Olga deserves better than the likes of you, and I'm here to make sure she gets it."

He whirled around and shouted, "Olga, I'm taking you to Doctor Taylor tomorrow morning so he can take care of your little indiscretion. After that, you'll be packed off to Stonehenge, a boarding college for young girls like yourself who need more structure and discipline. You whore! You rejected Tom Williams for this poor bastard! What the hell is wrong with you?"

Olga was hysterical and blurted out, "Daddy, we love each other!"

"Shut up, you disappointing slut," Murphy angrily interrupted. "You think I've worked this hard to get this farm to where it is today, so I can turn it over to the likes of this bloody bastard? I'd rather set it afire!"

Murphy aimed the gun at Olga and yelled, "I'll kill you too and get it over with. Do what I say, or it's over for both of you!"

"Run Ian, run," Olga screamed. "Get out of here before he kills us both!"

Ian bolted into the night. Halfway between

the main house and the compound, John and Christopher walked him back to their room in silence, except for the occasional, "Oh my God! Old Murphy is a dangerous man. Why'd you have to pick his daughter?"

An hour later, John and Christopher took Ian and his belongings three miles to John's mother's house. She offered to put him up for a couple of weeks until he decided what to do. Ian, tired and broken hearted, flopped down on the settee and did not move until the next morning.

Early on October 30, 1750, Ian woke up bruised, defeated and confused. He could not return to Stobhill; there was no opportunity there for a young man to make anything of his life. His father had just retired and could hardly make ends meet. Ian felt like a trapped animal, with nowhere to go and no future. Ben Murphy, well known in the area, would make sure Ian didn't get a job anywhere nearby.

On the third day John's mother said, "Ian, have you heard about what's going on in the islands of the West Indies? We Brits are colonizing them. I've read that we've taken over one island called Jamaica."

Ian looked up from his depression, "But hasn't Jamaica been under Spanish rule?"

"We've run the Spanish off to Cuba and I think Mexico," she said. "Many young Brits have been going there by ship to make a life for themselves. Some of them get jobs as overseers right away."

"Overseers right away? How is that possible?"

"There is a shortage of white men on the island. Those who have the courage to take the trip are welcomed and given the best jobs. It may not be a bad option for you right now!"

Ian began exploring the idea right away. He learned that a ship called The Flying Flamborough was due to sail to Jamaica in a week. The passage was 50 British pounds, and Ian had managed to save 200 pounds on Murphy's farm. On November 2, 1750, Ian sailed to Jamaica in the West Indies.

The trip was grueling and terrifying. When the crew and passengers finally arrived in the Caribbean Sea, pirates, menacing tropical storms, and a near mutiny onboard met them. Luckily, the pirates encountered were from British ships looking to raid Spanish galleons, so they were allowed to continue along their treacherous journey. One tropical storm tossed and bucked the ship through 15-foot waves. Crew and passengers screamed for relief, which they thought would never come.

Finally, after weeks of terror and uncertainty, just as Ian felt he had made a terrible decision that would cost him his life, he beheld an awesome sight in the distance — the coastline of the small island called Jamaica.

As the ship drew closer, Ian peered ahead at a land of great beauty, at mountains that cascaded dangerously down into the azure-blue sea, at miles and miles of white-sand beaches, and what from afar looked like rainforests. The sea was as clear as crystal. Ian felt like he could bend over and touch colorful tropical fish from the bow of the vessel that had brought him safely to the shores of a fascinating yet intimidating place. He remembered gloomy old England and thought what a great difference it would be to explore this exotic island.

Three days after Ian Reid reached Jamaica, he had secured a job as overseer at Susumbavale, an estate owned by wealthy British landowner, Clinton Vassell. The estate was located in an area called Trelawny on the island's north coast. With sheer delight, Ian knew his days as a farmhand were over. He was elated. Introduced around by Vassell, he was immediately welcomed into the small society of whites in the area.

The lifestyle in Jamaica was completely different. Ian quickly realized that to survive, he would have to adjust rapidly. The slave trade had brought thousands of Africans to work the plantations and estates. Despite his quick employment and promotion to overseer, the environment was harsh for any white person, a clear reason why there were so few of them on the island. Vassell told Ian that many had survived the rough voyage from England to Jamaica, only to succumb to vicious and mysterious tropical diseases.

Ian began hearing about the wrath of the

dreaded free blacks called Maroons, who lived in the hills of Jamaica and had made life a living hell for the landowners. Vassel told him the Maroons were notorious for violent attacks on the estates and plantations, killing whites and burning their properties to ashes. They incited the slaves to rebel and bolt. Those who lived to join the Maroons in the hills brought with them critical inside information. Ian saw obvious fear among his white friends as they talked about their plight and the dreaded Maroons.

With whites a tiny minority, Ian quickly learned that the only way for them to maintain any control was through brute force and intimidation. Slaves who unsuccessfully attempted to pull foot and bolt were brutally maimed and even burned at the stake as an example to other blacks that may get any ideas of rebellion and escape.

Ian performed his first slave punishment very soon after he started working at Susumbavale. Vassell's house slave, Unta, had been caught leaking information about the estate's occupants to one of the Maroon chiefs at nearby Maroon Town. One of Vassell's trusted overseers caught Unta trying to escape through the woods behind Susumbavale. He was brought back to the estate, dreading his certain fate.

Vassell, furious, also felt completely betrayed. "Take this as a lesson if you plan to survive in this treacherous place," Vassel told Ian. "You are about to exercise brute force over your first slave. They are all liars, cheats and animals that cannot be trusted for one minute. You will lash him 200 times across the back, after which I will rub salt, pepper and lime into his open wounds. Then you will cut his head off with this machete, and I will hang it in the town square for all to see."

"Why isn't the lashing enough?" Ian immediately asked.

"He was a trusted house slave," Vassel said. "He listened to my conversations around the dining table every night. He knows my secrets, business and personal. To have those leaked to the Maroons I cannot afford to take lightly. It could cost me my life; it could cost you your life."

Ian proceeded with the lashing and pretended that he was beating a most dangerous animal. He lashed Unta until he had ripped half the flesh off his back. He was amazed that throughout the lashing Unta showed no reaction to the fierce pain and degradation. Unta seemed to have allowed his soul to leave his body. "How could a human being bear such pain without screaming?" thought Ian. "They must really be animals."

Vassell approached with the mixture of salt, pepper and lime. He began viciously rubbing it onto Unta's bloody back. Unta spun around suddenly, eyes red, distorted with pain, and uttered a guttural growl. Then he spat directly into Vassell's face.

Vassel screamed with anger, "Cut his head off with the machete right now!"

So convinced that Unta was indeed an animal, Ian swung the machete and felt it hack through flesh and bone. He was astonished by the vengeance and satisfaction that he felt.

Unta's head hung in Trelawny's town square for weeks. His brutalized body was tossed out for the crows to devour. That type of brutality was not unusual for slaves who defied their masters. By the time Ian left Susumbavale, he had personally hacked and maimed many slaves unfortunate enough to be caught committing misdeeds."

I looked around and my sister Dahlia's face was distorted with fear and disgust. Both of Clinton's lips were shaking violently with disbelief. I felt like someone stabbed me in the gut with a sharp knife. I spun around and said, "My God, Sedith, how could they get away with killing and brutalizing human beings like that? Just listening to it makes me sick in the gut."

Sedith sighed and yelled, "Cookie, bring these children some hot Ovaltine and bread pudding. I think they need some comforting right now."

We took a break to sip on Cookie's hot Ovaltine, which was spiced with fresh vanilla, nutmeg and sweet condensed milk. Not a word was uttered. We were literally licking our wounds with the hot beverage. Just as I began to dread hearing anymore,

Sedith stared off into the distance once again. I resigned myself to the fact that more torture to my ears was coming, like it or not.

"The English women in Jamaica had obviously been raised with prudish attitudes toward sex, so it was not easy for a white man to get his needs met. Many nights Ian fought memories of his hot sexual romps with Olga in the haystacks of Murphy's horse barn. He longed to have her with him in Jamaica; but the thought that old man Murphy would breast stroke it all the way to Jamaica and chop off his head, just like he had just done to another of Vassell's slaves, wiped that wish right out of his mind.

Most white men were busy having sex with their female slaves in Jamaica, a behavior tolerated by other whites. It was expected. Many white men had multiple black and mulatto concubines. They also passed on many diseases to naïve and unsuspecting slave women.

The first time Ian ordered a mulatto slave named Idora to his quarters for sex, she attempted to walk away. He grabbed her by the hair with such violence and desire he again astonished himself. After that first act of sexual aggression, Idora became one of his concubines. She gave in to his demands to make her life a little easier.

When Ian Reid had five full years as an overseer at Susumbavale under his belt, he had saved a

substantial amount of money and had become
cold and brutal. He began looking for a plantation
of his own, and about a year later he traveled to
Portland Cottage, a little village in a desirable area,
Clarendon, close to a number of other plantations.
At that time, much of the land in the area was being
bought and transformed into lucrative sugarcane-
producing estates.

Jamaica had become one of the jewels of the
English crown, and sugar was the major income
generator. An estate in Portland Cottage called
Twickenham was for sale, and Ian went to look
at it. Twickenham's owner had recently died after
a long fight with malaria. His widow wanted to
return to England. Six weeks later, Ian Reid owned
Twickenham, 58 slaves, a charming great house, and
a thriving up-and-coming sugarcane business. He
immediately hired Bazil Dawkins, a local mulatto,
as his overseer. Bazil's beautiful young sister, Kiko,
became Ian's concubine and housemaid.

Kiko and Bazil were the children of a white
plantation owner in the area and a black slave.
Their slave-master father freed them before he died
of dysentery three years earlier. Ian did not know
that a significant Maroon presence had infiltrated
Clarendon. He also did not know that earlier Kiko
had a love affair with one of the most cantankerous
local Maroon chiefs, Juan Barbieri. Spaniards
had given many Maroons these names when

they colonized Jamaica. Some, including Juan, spoke fluent Spanish. Kiko and Juan had a son together. When she accepted work at Twickenham, she left the boy with Juan to be raised as a free Maroon. Kiko did not want her son anywhere near plantation life. Juan and Kiko had had a major disagreement before she left. Although he let her go, Juan was obviously still in love with her.

When Kiko arrived at Twickenham, she could not help but admire the splendid great house with five bedrooms, a vast living room filled with mahogany British colonial furniture, the lovely veranda that wrapped around the entire house, framed on the outside with gorgeous red, yellow and green crotons and flowering hibiscus. The back veranda looked over a beautiful clay pond. The pond's water was crystal clear, and Ian had begun to raise tropical freshwater fish as a hobby.

One step down from the pantry was a cool room paved with river rocks — a small, dark room that was Massa's wine cellar, lined with wines from all over the world. When Ian entertained, he proudly escorted guests through his fascinating house and finally to the wine cellar, bragging about the origins of his exotic collection. He asked a special guest to pick one or two bottles for the dinner table, and then he ordered Kiko to bring the bottle opener so he could do the honors. Ian poured a small stash into the glass of another lucky guest, for tasting *and comment. This was followed by an elaborate tropical meal prepared by Kiko.*

Ian's first five years as Twickenham's slave master were of fine living, prosperity and wealth, while the slaves toiled day and night in pain and exhaustion, savagely beaten and mutilated by Ian or his overseer for the slightest resistance. After all, to Ian that was how you kept the Negroes in line.

But many nights, the abeng horns pounded relentlessly from nearby Maroon villages. The black freedom fighters were inciting rebellion. The slaves looked around discreetly with hope and freedom in their heads. Ian increased the beatings and brutality.

Slaves lost legs or had their heads chopped off by Ian himself for responding to the call of the abeng. For other misdeeds, one arm would slowly be burned off, an eye gouged out, or 200 to 500 lashes were inflicted until the flesh fell off of the poor victims' backs. They kept on heeding the abeng's call and welcomed death over torture and degradation.

Ian was 32 years old when he married Wendy Powell, a frail white woman from nearby Mitchell Town. Her father owned the prestigious Appelgate Plantation. Now Ian had a wife and three concubines, including Kiko. Ian and Wendy named their son Trevor. The best slave midwife at Twickenham delivered him one hot July night. As

Trevor grew into adolescence, many said he thrived under savagery and rampant brutality. Young Trevor whipped the slaves and ordered mutilations on those who attempted to pull foot and bolt. It became a way of life for him; it was all that he knew. Ian had schooled him well.

Ian Reid died of malaria at age 53 when his son was barely 20 years old. As Twickenham's slave master, Trevor already had an ugly reputation for arrogance, cruelty and sexual tyranny against any young slave girl chosen as his latest conquest. Twickenham had become the plantation most slaves dreaded! But not far away, the haunting abeng horn blasted louder and louder. The pulsating rhythms of Maroon drums pounded relentlessly under the vengeful direction of Maroon Chief Juan and of his and Kiko's son, Kinto.

Reid had precisely programmed his son Trevor in the cruelties of slave mastering. Juan had rigorously trained his son's mind and body on the rigors of black resistance against the barbarism and cruelty of slavery.

chapter 5

Power + Passion = Rage

AWESTRUCK, AMUSED, JARRED, DEEPLY disturbed — these feelings taunted us the week after Sedith's last stories, and we were unable to stop discussing them.

We chatted and lamented about the goriness and erotica. We were too preoccupied to climb trees or gallop through Twickenham. The foundation to the old great house took on new meaning now. The saga that just seemed to hurl at us, riveted us. The story was not over. We were hooked, and more tales were to come — I could feel it.

Sedith eyeballed us with wonder and concern. We assured her that we were OK; but we kept on whispering and reminiscing. We needed to get it out of our system before the next round of revelations. We were anxious, yet eager; but we were ready for the old lady to tell us more.

And soon enough the great narrator seared our young minds with a saga of violence, rage and deliverance. A week later, she gathered us together for another history lesson, this one in the form of a field trip. "We're going to the poinciana tree next to the old great house," she announced. "Cookie," she yelled, "bring two old blankets, the picnic baskets with lunch, and a dozen ripe mangoes. And don't forget the jug of brown-sugar lemonade. We'll be gone all afternoon!"

We sat gingerly down under the tree, our bodies instinctively facing remnants of the old great house. I glanced up — the poinciana was in full bloom. An overlay of red velvety blossoms sheltered our eager skulls from the warm afternoon sun. None of us jostled for position this time around.

Sedith began, much to our delight and chagrin. We were still a little troubled by the last stories.

"Trevor Reid took the helm of Twickenham at the tender age of 20, but there was nothing tender about Reid. He was raised to relish cruelty and destruction against mankind. And with a father capable of such cold and calculated behavior, Trevor never knew what it was like to be nurtured, let alone loved.

After all, Ian Reid had coldly sold his own mulatto children born from slave mistresses. As a youngster, Trevor watched with interest as his half brothers and sisters were bartered off like widgets in the open-slave market. He also listened keenly to the desperate pleas of their abused and distraught mothers, who were forced to look on as the slave trader's gavel pounded to close the sale. Trevor overheard the slaves talking about one of his father's slave mistresses, a woman named Elia. So traumatized, she murdered her own child immediately after birth to spare him the pain. She couldn't watch her boy be negotiated at a price to the next planter. So death was a better alternative.

One could clearly see the coldness in Trevor Reid's steely and emotionless blue eyes. He was programmed to believe in the inferiority of Africans. And this emotional warp also fueled his desire to rape and torture slave women."

"Jesus!" Dahlia groaned with revulsion. "How much worse can this get?"

"Much worse, me girl. Don't call the Lord's name in vain." responded Sedith. Then she pressed on.

"Trevor buried his father Ian without shedding a tear. This was how he sent his mother off to hell or glory three years earlier when she died from a mysterious fever. Convinced that his mother was poisoned by one of the house slaves, he could not prove it, so he had even more hate in his heart. He and his father eventually tortured and killed both house slaves in a vengeful rage. With his father gone, he was now free to run Twickenham with as much brutality as he dared to conjure up.

One of Trevor's first control tactics was to rid Twickenham of older, less productive slaves from his father's regime. These depreciating assets were sold at bargain prices to work as house slaves for other planters. To the buyers, these old laborers were well-trained, brainwashed, and far less likely to leak critical dining room talk to the Maroons.

After bartering off the old assets, Trevor traveled to the slave-trade market nearby. He bought 15 newly arrived Mandingo-type males and eight young females. The females looked strong enough to work the cane fields and bear children, he reasoned. But three of the 15 young males heeded the abeng horn immediately upon setting foot onto Twickenham. They pulled foot and bolted to the Maroon village nearby.

And information continued to leak from Twickenham's great house. The Maroons were quickly briefed on all activities around Reid's latest slave-trading activity. "Damn it," thought Trevor, "that was why the abeng blasted as the new slaves arrived." This was enough reason for him to go on another furious rampage, beating and torturing any slave who crossed his path. Still he could not expose the culprit. This stubborn passive resistance, Trevor thought, had turned slaves into particularly dangerous assets. He continued to conjure up more vengeful scourges that would protect his life and livelihood.

Reid was experiencing a level of resistance at

Twickenham that was beyond anything that existed during his father's days. One reason for this was the infusion of new Mandingos, who were masters at inciting the more seasoned slaves into trickery and rebellion. These resistance efforts, Trevor confided to his friend Charles Bailey, were wearing him down. Punishment no longer hampered the slaves' defiance and determination. Parts of the sugarcane crops would mysteriously disappear. Orders would be purposefully carried out incorrectly. Slowdowns were frequent. Faked illnesses were rampant. And the latest prank was the re-opening of old wounds to remove any ability to work for many more weeks. All of this had made a huge mark on slowing production down.

Trevor was aware that Jamaica held the record for slave revolts and Maroon warfare in the entire Caribbean. Not a day went by without some act of violence by a group of people who refused to accept slavery or any notion that they were inferior in any way, shape or form. One reason was the strong concentration of blacks born in free Maroon societies, and who were programmed from childhood in bush warfare. The other reason for this was the island's terrain. Jamaica's many mountains, rainforests and caves made it possible for frequent attacks against the plantations to be successful.

Trevor Reid had very few friends. This was not only because of his coldness, but also due to the fact that there were only a small number of whites in the area. Distressed about his current dilemma, he confided to his only friend Charles Bailey.

"I've thought of going to England," he told Charles, "but doubt that I could survive there. Jamaica is where I was born — this is my life. As uncivilized as it is here at times, this is all I know; but it is becoming more dangerous by the minute. New Maroon communities keep forming in the area, and there is not one slave at Twickenham that I can trust for even a minute."

Charles listened attentively, and replied, "What a lonely and terrifying existence you've carved out for yourself, old chap. Anyway you could be a little less harsh to a few of your slaves and try to win them over?" Charles continued with a wee bit of British arrogance that was beginning to annoy Trevor. "Daddy treats his three house slaves very well and is even able to get information from them about any potential plans to revolt or bolt."

"Charles, old boy, I've definitely burned all of those bridges," Trevor responded to this the only way he knew how to. "None of my slaves are stupid enough to have one iota of trust in me. When the new slaves join the others, they are immediately told what to expect from me, 'the wicked massa.' And they are always wondering what kind of cruelty I'll throw in their faces next."

So Charles asked, "What are you going to do?"

"Don't know this minute," Trevor replied, *with determination,* *"But until I've figured things out, there's no other way to ensure survival except by force, threats, intimidation and brutality."* Then he looked straight past Charles with those steely blue eyes and continued. *"When the Spanish brought these Kromantis into Jamaica, they didn't know it then, but they were giving us Brits one final, terrible blow before we ran them off to Cuba."*

"They must be laughing at us in their graves, those bastards!" he commented in cruel amusement. Trevor seemed regretful for the first time in his life.

Meanwhile, Maroon presence continued to build in the hills of Clarendon. The freedom fighters were beginning to target plantations reputedly run by the most cruel slave masters. Twickenham was on the targeted list, and Juan and Kiko's son, Kinto, was paying very close attention to Reid.

"Sounds like things are about to get rough at Twickenham, Sedith," Clinton interjected. "We all know that Kinto had a real axe to grind with Trevor Reid."

"Yes me boy," Sedith acknowledged. Then she continued. *"Kinto grew up listening to his father's account of how his mother was seduced by Ian Reid, and how Reid raped her repeatedly 'till she had no choice but to succumb to his sadistic tirades. Kinto was also told that he had one mulatto brother and a sister born of Reid and his mother. They were both sold in the slave market to planters from another island. As a teenager, Kinto secretly wished he knew where his siblings were. He hoped that he would be able to free them and bring them back to Jamaica one day."*

"Unbelievable how families were torn apart under slavery," Dahlia commented. "And how more sad can it get — slave women choosing to murder their own children rather than put them through this torture. I'm getting sick to the stomach."

"I know child," our grandmother responded. "But you must continue to listen carefully." Then she proceeded.

"One of the female slaves Trevor Reid just bought was a beautiful 16-year-old girl. Reid named her Petra, and he had been keeping a close eye on her over the year that she worked the fields. He planned to make her a house slave and one of his concubines very soon. Petra was a mixture of black and Arawak Indian. She had beautiful smooth brown skin and long, curly, dark brown hair that cascaded down her back in an ample braid. She was a sight to behold."

"Oh boy, here we go again," Clinton exclaimed. "Sedith, is there more sex talk coming our way?"

"No boy. But I'm sure you'd love to hear more of that talk, you little rat!" the old lady responded, slightly amused. She was relentless now with the story, so no time was wasted as she looked off into the sunset and continued.

"*Unknown to Trevor, during her first year as a field slave, Petra was one of the primary informants to Kiko's Maroon camp. She was also meeting secretly with Kinto. They had romantic feelings for each other. At that time, it was not unusual for Maroon men and slave women to develop intimate ties, and for their children to be sold at very high prices in the slave markets. But Petra managed to get by undetected. Her good looks had helped her avoid many of Reid's lashings for petty infractions. And Kinto was planning a future with her as soon as he had enough inside information on Twickenham to do some real damage.*

Very soon Petra reached the age of 17. Trevor ordered her out of the cane fields to become the house slave who prepared his meals and cleaned his bedroom. She immediately knew what this meant and was sickened by the thought of Reid's cruel hands anywhere near her.

She sent a message to Kinto, whose response sickened her even more. Kinto told her to move into Twickenham's great house with Reid and get all the information she could to him. He was both disgusted and enraged. Kinto went into a jealous rage and carefully plotted revenge on Reid for taking his woman. Not only would he get Petra, he would finally free all slaves from Reid's clutches.

"Reid will suffer!" swore Kinto. "I will kill him myself!"

Petra was soon moved into Twickenham's great house. That first night there, Reid ordered her to scrub his back in the bath pan. He was stark naked — a kerosene lamp burned dimly nearby. She winced when he stroked her breast. He slapped her abruptly. He tied her arms to the bedpost. He humped her like she had no soul. Petra closed her eyes. She mentally removed her soul from her body. She survived the pain and humiliation. Then later she learned to do this very well. Now she had developed two selves — her physical self without soul and her emotional self.

"I thought you said there was no more of this talk coming?" Clinton grinned.

"Didn't want to disappoint my lovely and curious grandson," Sedith responded. Then she persisted with the story.

"*Petra relentlessly continued to sneak information to Kinto; but she grieved each day and wondered when Kinto would come to rescue her. She gathered all the strength it took and hung on to the faith that freedom was coming, one way or another.*

One Friday evening, Petra was to be lashed by Reid for supposedly flirting with a young Mandingo slave. Actually, she was passing information to Kinto through him; but Reid's jealousy and ego took over. He was blinded to what was truly taking place. Petra did the usual. She removed her soul from her body and took the whipping.

Six months later she was pregnant with Reid's child. Petra had already decided that she would kill herself and the child rather than watch him sold at the slave auction. She told this to Reid. To her surprise, he assured her that she could keep the child. Petra wondered why she was being made this promise. Massa was famous for selling the children of his slaves and replacing them with outsiders. No one was allowed any family relationships at Twickenham. Still, Petra struggled to be happy. It was indeed a struggle, as guilt at the thought of other slave mothers who suffered day and night overwhelmed her.

She also wondered about Kinto. How will he feel about her expecting Reid's child? Could Reid be in love with her? She wiped that thought from her mind immediately. "That cold white man is not capable of any love," she thought. What was she thinking? Confusion and guilt again took over. She couldn't get the other slave women out of her mind. Standing there, arms outstretched as the slave trader's hammer slammed their babies away forever. Then they were hurried away, eyes vacant, souls ripped out of their bodies. They would toil in the cane fields afterwards, like animals without hearts. They were grateful for the numbness. Feelings came with excruciating pain.

"This must have been devastating!" Dahlia

grieved. But the old lady continued without a comment.

"Petra's son was born one hot August night. She pushed him from her loins, gripping the bedpost with one hand, clutching the hand of the slave midwife with the other. The midwife handed Petra her newborn mulatto baby. There was a look of envy and disdain in the old woman's eyes. This look haunted Petra for months, because what it said without a doubt was the following. "You opportunistic slut ... you sleep with the cruel white man and now you are the only one on this plantation allowed to keep your child. If I had my way, I would kill you both."

For Petra, the only thing worse than the physical pain of childbirth was worry about her son's future. The new mother promised herself she would do whatever it took to give him a life of freedom. She would make sure he knew what dignity felt like. She named him Andrew. Reid's interest in the child was minimal; but she was allowed to keep and care for him, so she gave gratefulness a shot.

A violent and deadly slave rebellion, masterminded by the Maroons, had destroyed Clarendon's largest sugarcane plantation nearby. All 500 slaves on that plantation participated. Hundreds escaped and joined the Maroons in the mountains of Clarendon. They were welcomed and trained in guerilla warfare. They helped form a social order that exists even today in the hills of Jamaica. This big Clarendon revolt paved the way for a stronger community of freedom fighters, which encouraged more cultural unity among the Maroons.

Escapees from other African tribes would proudly hail themselves as Kromantis. After all, the traders were famous for touting their slaves as Kromantis to demand the highest price. Why shouldn't escaped slaves now use this as a means of solidarity, cultural unification, and terror to the planters? In Jamaica, the common and brutal experience of slavery served as the foundation for brotherhood and solidarity among Kromantis ... slaves ... escapees ... and now Maroons.

"Yes, yes!" Clinton yelled, jumping up and down again, fist in the air.

"Calm down boy ... stop acting like a raging Maroon," Sedith teased. Then she continued.

"Trevor Reid was visibly shaken by the news about this huge and bloody rebellion in the area. He heard that the plantation owner and all overseers were massacred. He also heard that the fields were slashed and burned to ashes. Reid summoned his friend Charles to Jackson's Bay Beach next door.

As he paced back and forth agitatedly in the white sand, face flushed with fear, he told Charles, "It is getting overly treacherous, old chap. The Maroons have increased their presence and stronghold in the area. Every single one of my 86 slaves is incited and ready to pull foot and bolt. I can see it in their eyes. We've had to increase lashings for lollygagging and whispering. It has gotten so bad I cannot dare trust the mother of my own child. How have you been coping with the situation?"

"We are all terrified, Trevor," Charles replied. "Daddy has also grown to distrust his house slaves, and we can't decide whether to overlook minor infractions and treat them better or to brutalize their backsides." Charles continued, his eyes now filled with regret. "We have taken their souls by enslaving and brutalizing them. Now it is almost impossible to read them. The most trusted slave, who cooks for your family, serves you at the table, takes care of your children when they are sick, could turn on you the next minute. We have created monsters, and we may pay for this with our lives."

"But they are supposed to be like animals, without the intelligence it requires to form the alliances that are now threatening our mere existence!" Trevor responded, with much trepidation.

"Ah Trevor," Charles groaned. "We convinced ourselves that they are animals to justify the beatings and brutality. We did it to control them. We were always terrified of them. This fear has turned us into cruel animals ourselves."

"What is your family going to do?" asked a despondent Trevor. "I hear talk that the government

is planning to try and negotiate a peace treaty with certain Maroon communities. This would be a good thing, I suppose. But we've abused the slaves so much I don't think any peace treaty will take away the pain and vengefulness we are responsible for placing in their hearts."

"We will either have to return to the mother country or wait and see what happens," sighed a very tired Charles. "In the meantime, Trevor, I suggest that you find a way to make peace with at least a few of your slaves. How about Petra ... could you use her as a conduit to some kind of peace with the others? After all, she is the mother of your son. And you did allow her to keep the boy!"

"I don't know, Charles." Trevor sighed with doubt and fear. "Petra looks at me with dead eyes. I also created that monster. Maybe we should all pull foot like the slaves say, find our relatives in England, and beg them to take us in," he said. "You've heard of the beatings the British Redcoats have gotten from the Maroon guerillas. We Brits don't want to admit it, but the Maroons have won hands-down in every battle against the British army."

"I know," Charles added. "Brits are not equipped to fight in this type of environment and terrain. By the time the Redcoats fire one round blindly from their bayonets and retreat to reload, the Maroons descended upon them like vultures disguised as tropical foliage, chopping off heads and downing

those who flee with bows and arrows. They are fierce, cunning and precise fighters."

"We are all doomed, Charles." Trevor was defeated now, as he continued. "With one man to every five Redcoats, the Maroons have defied us and whipped the backsides out of Great Britain, the world's great power. How the hell did we allow this to happen?"

Charles attempted to calm him down, but to no avail. Trevor continued, "Have you heard that one successful Maroon raid against us was led by a woman 'Chieftainess' named Nanny? A woman led a successful Maroon rebellion against us, for God's sake!"

"Yes … teacher Williams taught us about Nanny last week," Clinton yelled. "A Maroon woman kicked their backsides!" Clinton kept interrupting, despite threats from Sedith; but the old lady pressed on.

"Go home Trevor and attempt to mend some fences if you can," Charles responded with exhaustion. "None of us have any of the answers at this time!"

But Trevor, who was still visibly agitated and frightened, continued, "And they have also brought some kind of voodoo with them from Africa called Obeah. There are Obeah men everywhere who are supposed to heal the sick and put hexes on the evil. They are some evil and scary-looking bastards — have you ever seen one of them? Sometimes I feel like a bloody hex has been put on me."

I elbowed Clinton on the down low. He and I had already seen the Obeah man at work. I returned to the story ... Sedith was relentless with it.

"And the Maroons, many who speak fluent Spanish from the days of Spanish domination, have now declared that free blacks should be speaking some kind of Jamaican language, a mixture of English, African tribal languages, and a little Spanish," Trevor continued, now with even more angst. "My slaves are beginning to speak it. Now I cannot understand what the hell they are saying!"

Trevor was on target about the Obeah men and their influence on the slaves. Completely stripped of any personal as well as civil rights, many slaves turned to the type of Afro-Caribbean religious practices that were totally foreign to Brits. Most religious practices were organized in secret. These rituals offered a strong support for resistance. They made the slaves feel internally empowered. This was fully embraced in a time of abuse and domination.

Obeah became a powerful tool of black control and retribution against the massa. Whites may have died of natural causes or from disease; but the slave believed the Obeah man had done his work and done it very well. Teacher Williams may have taught you that most slave and Maroon rebellions on the island included the Obeah man, who sometimes led the uprisings. They were great at building confidence in an oppressed and abused people. They would convince the black warriors of their invincibility if they practiced certain religious rituals before going to war."

"Wow!" Clinton exclaimed, winking at me. Sedith didn't respond and continued without pause.

"The slaves also relieved stress and empowered themselves through music and dance. And no matter how hard the planters tried to suppress and control their covert efforts to entertain and empower themselves, they persisted out of necessity. It was another way to maintain their sanity. So when the massa took away all the drums and ordered other handmade musical instruments to be burned, they would dance and sing to the distant drums of the Maroons. Resistance in any form was better than no resistance at all. And this served as a constant reminder of how fragile the slave master's methods of control had become. It was also a reminder that there were free blacks nearby, whose ranks the slaves would attempt to join sooner, rather than later."

"My God, Sedith. These were some strong and determined people," Dahlia exclaimed. "What happened next?"

"Total mayhem and destruction would loom over Twickenham next, me girl," Sedith responded as she resumed her story.

"It came swiftly and violently. On a hot-and-tranquil night in late August, the plantation was fully operational. Slaves labored by torch light,

squeezing the liquid from freshly cut sugarcane before fermentation could set in. It was common for them to toil 18 to 20 hours per day, first in the boiling sun, and then at night, while fanning mosquitoes and hoping for some much-needed rest. Petra was in the great house preparing dinner for Reid and his three overseers. She suddenly looked up, startled. The abeng horn just made three distinct blasts. Then she heard rhythmic drums pounding louder and louder. There was an eerie uniqueness about the sounds tonight. Then the horn gave six more blasts, three long spurts at a time. In the background, drums pounded louder and louder, until they came to a frightening pitch. This was definitely a distinct rhythm that Petra had not heard before. She hurled Andrew up in her arms and dashed to the front door. She was stopped dead in her tracks by an alarming spectacle ahead.

All slaves were at full attention staring in the direction of the horns and drums. They were ready to pull foot and bolt. Then an explosion jolted her. Stinging heat enveloped her body. To her right in the distance were Reid and one overseer galloping toward the great house, whips hurriedly thrown to the ground behind them. Suddenly, out of nowhere, tropical foliage moved, became denser, and surrounded Twickenham like a shroud of condemnation. Another thick forest had slowly moved in on Petra and Andrew.

Petra stared ahead to behold slaves grabbing work-light torches and setting everything around them ablaze. Then they pulled foot and bolted out into the night. The forest quickly parted to let them through. Ear-piercing screams, agonizing jolts, drums pounding incessantly — that's all Petra heard now. Little Andrew covered his ears in horror. A fast-moving coconut tree hacked off the head of one of Reid's mulatto overseers whose name was Peter. Petra slammed her eyes shut to shun that horror. Reid was now a few feet from the veranda. A pineapple bush leapt from the shadows and grabbed him by the throat. Behind him, a head went flying by trailed by blood and more gore. It was the head of overseer John, a Brit. A croton bush in arms beheaded him. Now Petra squinted to see through the blood that confronted her.

"Don't kill him!" Petra howled, eyes riveted on Reid's frantic face.

She immediately saw Kinto's sweaty and frenzied eyes staring down at her from the pineapple bush. His machete was ready to do its work on Reid's throat. Petra again yelped, "Don't let Andrew see you chop him up, pleeeaaase!"

Andrew, looking on in terror, clutched his mother's neck and let out an ear-piercing wail. Kinto let go of Reid, scooped Petra and Andrew up, and disappeared with them into the night. With a hot breeze fanning her ears, Petra glanced back

*to behold the cane fields of Twickenham burning
brightly under the dark, smoke-filled tropical
skies. She had just witnessed the end of a cruel and
unbearable era."*

"What happened next, Sedith? Tell us now!" I
said. We were all jumping up and down like daunted
Maroons. Sedith pressed on relentlessly. She was
fueled by our awe once more.

*"Several days later, a runaway slave from
Twickenham showed up at Kinto's hut and handed
Petra a small, brown paper bag. She quickly opened
it to find the papers for Twickenham. There was
a simple note attached in what looked like Reid's
handwriting. The note said "for Andrew Reid."
Petra couldn't read it, but she got the message.
Later, she heard that the estate of Reid's friend
Charles also suffered a devastating Maroon attack;
but Reid and Charles managed to get away. The two
were able to board a ship headed for England.*

"My name is Edith Reid," Sedith stood up and
dramatically declared. We looked up in amazement
as she continued. "Twickenham is now mine, and I
will pass it onto you, my beloved grandchildren. Let
no one ever take it away from you."

Then before we could take our bottom lips up off
the ground, our grandmother quickly grabbed an
old, tattered history book from her picnic basket
and said, "Maroon attacks on plantations continued
in full force all over Jamaica after Twickenham fell."

Then she buried her face into the book and began reading out loud, just like Parson Mitchell would read the tattered old Bible to us in church. "The British Army, despite many gallant attempts, failed to rid the island of the black freedom fighters. Special slave hunters with bloodhounds from Cuba and Miskito Indians from Central America were brought in; but the Maroons, though under greater pressure, continued to assert their right to co-existence.

"The Maroons eventually signed a peace treaty with the British. This guaranteed their freedom, gave them specific rights as free citizens, and called a halt to the hostilities. They are credited with the reason that slavery was abolished in Jamaica. This abolition finally came in the early-to-mid 1800s.

"After slavery ended, many of the planters attempted to coerce the freed slaves into continuing to work on the plantations. Most of them refused and took to the hills, where they occupied plots of land, built huts, and started their own cultivation of fruits, vegetables and foodstuff. They rounded up family members who were sold to other planters and helped get them on their feet. Many combined wage labor with their farming and survived quite well.

"Sugar production now rapidly declined, and the banana industry began to rise substantially. This was good for freed blacks that now had their own plots of land. Bananas could be grown on small plots as well as large estates.

"The planters were now desperate to find labor. They began importing thousands of indentured laborers from India to fill the gap. Then came an influx of Jews, Syrians, Chinese and Portuguese to the island."

Sedith then looked at us and announced, "Your aunt's friends, the Issas and Chungs, are descendants of these immigrants." Our grandmother then buried her head back into the book and continued reading out loud. "The Jamaican urban middle class was also occupied by mulattos or light-skinned descendants of master and slave, many of whom were also farmers.

"After slavery Jamaica was being run by the local elite, with Britain stepping in only occasionally to ensure protection of its interests. And though blacks were now free, they had no political rights. Of course, this was completely unacceptable to Jamaicans. So more rebellions and rioting continued as they relentlessly fought for more rights. One famous rebellion took place in the late 1800s."

Sedith looked up at us again and asked, "Remember teacher Williams telling you about our national hero named Paul Bogel? He led a rebellion that left a few dozen people killed. The white powers-that-be reacted hysterically. Out of fear, they held military trials and severely punished hundreds of participants and sympathizers of the rebellion. According to the history books, over 1,000 blacks were either hanged or flogged in response. And the houses of over another 1,000 blacks were burned to the ground; but the fight continued as black Jamaicans, now free to maneuver, refused to accept anything less than equal rights and justice for all. Though painful, these rebellions shocked the British into coming to terms with the fact that change was needed. They also resulted in the formation of one of our first political parties, the People's National Party or PNP."

Sedith walked us home at dusk in silence, with the fireflies lighting our paths. Then she fondled our awestruck faces and ordered us to bed. Exhaustion set in, and I drifted off to sleep, determined that I needed her to take me through Twickenham tomorrow afternoon for another look at the old great house foundation and all that surrounded it. That night I dreamed of slave uprisings, Maroon courage, piercing machetes coming out of the dark from banana stalks, thunder, lightening, great fires singeing my skin. It was worse than one of Parson Mitchell's brimstone-and-fire nightmares.

What a defining day that was for me!

chapter 6

Sedith And
Her Brood

*T*HROUGH ELEGANCE AND HARDSHIP, Sedith worked hard to maintain one despite the other. She raised four children, held her head high, clutched onto her status as Portland Cottage's matriarch, and always kept a stiff upper lip.

Sedith's husband died in 1930. Alone, she raised four active children — and single parenting was far from fashionable in those days. Born Edith Reid of privileged background she married George Jennings. He was a sugar-factory manager whose work took him all over the island. Despite rumors that George had another family in St. Thomas, the other side of the island where he worked, Sedith chose to ignore them and immerse herself into church, child-rearing and managing Twickenham. At times, she was so alone. It was not easy raising

Sybil, George, Aubrey and Clovis without a father. Clovis, nicknamed Mass Pet, was the youngest of her brood and my beloved father. By the time her husband died, Sedith was already an experienced single parent. After all, he was rarely around; but she was not prepared for parenting and no financial support from a working husband. There was lots of land but very little money.

Sedith made a living selling fresh fruit and provisions grown at Twickenham. On Wednesday evenings, the market women would arrive in noisy, old trucks and donkey carts. They bought food and fruit just in time for the weekend market bustle in May Pen, a nearby town. Twickenham's Busha, Mista Mack, was frequently in charge. He was working for a busy widow with little time for the details. So Mista Mack made sure he got his share of profits under the table. The old slave mentality of trickery was still alive in him. He bartered openly with the market women, declaring, "Buy the Bombay mango for five shillings a dozen, and I'll give you the Julie mango for three shillings a dozen." Of course, proceeds from the latter sale went into his pocket.

Mass Pet, a rebel and the youngest of Sedith's brood, took it on himself to help feed the family. Fishing, bagging sea turtles, shooting wild ducks in the bushes of Twickenham — this was how he spent his afternoons after school. And because of this, Sedith had abundance at the dinner table. She also had enough to feed many of the town's less fortunate who showed up on her veranda.

Mass Pet was the most handsome of Sedith's children. With straight, black shoulder-length hair and a thin, muscular build, he was a looker. Sedith's other children were more conventional and well behaved. Two of them could pass as whites. One was Aubrey, who became one of the island's most prominent scholars and accountants. The other was Sybil, who worked in Kingston as a dressmaker for the city's elite. She also socialized with their sons and daughters. George was as an auditor for WISCO, the island's most prominent sugar factory. My father dropped out of college much to Sedith's chagrin; but he became a self-taught engineer, architect, artist, guitarist and world traveler.

There he was, sitting under a poinciana tree, strumming his guitar, and singing melodically, "Brown skin gal stay home and mind baby, brown skin gal stay home and mind baby, Papa gone abroad, in a sailing boat, and 'till he come back home, stay home and mind baby!" This was my first memory of Mass Pet.

At three years old, I would stare adoringly into his deep-brown eyes. To me, he was an East Indian prince — with more exotic features, though. His mix of black, white and East Indian was responsible for those remarkable looks. He was my hero.

Mass Pet's friends were from the bushes. What a thorn this was in Sedith's side. They lived in thatch huts with outhouses. Other friends skillfully balanced buckets of water on their heads as they rode bicycles home. He was a rebellious advocate for the underdog. I watched Mass Pet build a concrete blockhouse for the least fortunate of his friends, Rough Scully. I would beg him to take me to the building site, with Sedith venting her disapproval. After a day of digging and nailing lots of cement blocks with rows of jutting steel, we would sit by the fire and gobble down curried chicken and dumplings out of chipped aluminum bowls. Then Mass Pet would boastfully challenge the group, "Who thinks they can beat me at dominoes?"

The women slurped sweet brown-sugar lemonade and watched their men slam the last domino with winning glee. They gossiped in Patois and let out big guffaws of bellyaching laughs at the latest village news.

Affectionately called the "unconventional rogue" by his siblings, Sedith could set no boundaries within which Mass Pet would comply. Every young woman in Portland Cottage and nearby towns would vie for his attention. Sedith said he had given her lots of gray hairs; but he was the one child she could depend on to ensure the family and neighbors in need ate heartily. George, Aubrey and Sybil were too busy being scholars and socialites to pay attention.

According to Mass Pet, the family's elitist attitude was nothing but "foolishness" when money was so scarce. To him, since "we cannot eat the land, we should use it fully to feed the family." Afternoons would find him navigating through Twickenham armed with a shotgun, shoulder bag to hold the latest catch, fishing lines and net — and in the end, there would be enough meat and fish to feed both family and the needy for a week. This, and the cassavas, yams and potatoes grown by Mista Mack, made for healthy eating. Dessert included plums, mangoes, naseberries and other tropical fruit fresh off the trees.

Aunt Sybil was beautiful and voluptuous. She was very light skinned, with straight black hair down to her waist. During her dressmaking days, it was fashionable for women to have custom-made clothes. So life as a dressmaker to Kingston's elites was exciting and lucrative. She outfitted their daughters and dated their sons. She would be driven to Portland Cottage by her latest suitor, armed with niceties in a cooler for the family. Always thrilled to see her, she was obviously the apple of Sedith's eyes. The whiter the man she arrived with, the more thrilled Sedith became. Mass Pet would taunt, "The old colonialist mentality is still rampant among us Jamaicans these days, isn't it? My mother, is this the reason your eyes light up when Sybil arrives with another white man?"

Sedith responded disapprovingly, "Pet, one day you're going to get yourself in some hot water if you don't stop flapping those lips of yours!"

One visit had Aunt Sybil screeching with disgust during dinner. She leaped over the family pet, Brutus, bolted to her bedroom, and tried to sweeten the air with short sprays from her expensive perfume bottle. Mass Pet laughed and commented, "My sister, are you too sophisticated to smell the fart of the family's pet?" Loud laughter and more of Sedith's disapproving looks followed.

Uncle Aubrey settled in Kingston after finishing college. He had a good life as one of the city's renowned accountants. He married Pearl Williams, who came from Kingston's high society. His visits to Portland Cottage were infrequent, because his wife didn't wish to spend so much time in the "bushes."

A "co-dependent lush" is how one could describe George or "Uncle Bugs" as we called him. He was a well-respected auditor who never left his mother's home. Neither did he marry. So Sedith took care of him while he provided for her financial needs during her later years. It was a good arrangement, but a Jamaican man who could "hold his liquor" was much revered by peers during those days. And the liquor was 180-proof pure Jamaican rum, which Uncle Bugs guzzled down at his favorite rum bar each evening. When he was too smashed to make it home, a very pretty East Indian barmaid nicknamed Quattie, would put him up for the night. Uncle Bugs and Quattie became quite an item. She let him have all the rum he wanted. Then it was off to her bed for lovemaking and passing out.

On an occasional night, we might hear someone yelling at Twickenham's gate, "Sedith, Mass Bugs' car is parked by Jackson's Bay Beach, and he's fast asleep in it!"

Sedith and I would take the two-mile trek to Jackson's Bay. Then I'd cautiously drive the car home in first gear. At seven years old, I didn't know how to shift gears. One night on our walk home from church with the fireflies circling ahead, Sedith turned her flashlight to the left and exclaimed, "But stop, Miss Olivia, doesn't that look like Bugs' car?"

So once again, I was taking the first-gear drive home with the driver's door open, one foot on the ground, Sedith hanging onto the door trotting and warning, "Take it easy, child, before the car runs away with you."

Once home, Sedith opened Twickenham's large iron gates as I navigated the car close to the veranda. We would drag Uncle Bugs from the car, undress him, and put him to bed while he giggled, stared at Sedith in a stupor and mumbled, "How's my miserable church mouse of a mother tonight?" Before Sedith could vent her disgust, loud snores filled the room as the liquor got the best of him.

Sedith eventually buried him. He was the only child she was forced to endure the pain of laying to rest. He died at a young age from cirrhosis of the liver. And Quattie, the barmaid, sang a loud-and-screeching hymn at his graveside.

Mass Pet was the only one of Sedith's brood to leave the island in search of fortune and adventure. His first trip was to London by ship. He secured a job there with an engineering firm that deployed men all over Europe, the Middle East and North Africa to work on special projects in factories, and even on oil rigs in the Black Sea. He would return to Jamaica after eight-month stints bearing silks from Bombay, rugs from Morocco, and other exciting wares.

But the most exciting gifts he brought were stories of fascinating lands. How he hunted and ate hedgehogs with his English buddies and pretended he was eating a fresh chicken from Twickenham. Or how, on a trip to a small village in the Czech Republic, the villagers hurried around just to touch him — they had never before seen dark-skinned people. While we listened with wide-eyed wonder, Uncle Bugs would mumble between sips of rum chased with cow's milk "to coat his stomach," "Pet, you too rass (Jamaican expletive) lie." We would roar with laughter as Sedith, the "church mouse" looked on disapprovingly.

chapter 7

Miss Birdie

$\mathcal{M}$Y MOTHER MISS BIRDIE WAS GLAMOROUS, unconventional, passionate and conflicted. At times she balanced these traits well. Most of the time, these qualities worked together against both reason and logic.

She was from a unique background. She was born Isma Cole in Kingston — or Isma Thomas, depending on whether she was being acknowledged by her mother or father. Miss Birdie was blessed or felt burdened with two last names. The child of a white mother and black father, both parents registered her with their own family name. Why did this happen? A racial family feud resulted in her mother being pressured to give her the Thomas name. When her father discovered this, he went to the authorities and registered her with his own last name. This was the beginning of a long and complicated family saga.

Miss Birdie's mother and family moved to Jamaica from England in 1914. They were the Thomases from Brighton with two brothers, three sisters, a mother and father. The island was a British Colony then, with the national anthem of "God Save the Queen" and currency of pounds, shillings and pence. During those days, British migrants enjoyed the best of what Jamaica had to offer. Along with Syrian, Lebanese and Chinese immigrants, they owned the island's most profitable businesses and enjoyed lavish homes. These businesses included stores, supermarkets and resort hotels on the beautiful North Coast. And their homes had all luxuries, including maids, gardeners and chauffeurs.

The Thomases lived in a modest home in one of Kingston's upscale neighborhoods. They were not at all wealthy. Grand Uncle Patrick helped support the family by working as administrative director for the nearby psychiatric hospital. His brother Eric owned a small shoe repair shop two miles from home. The three girls, Violet, Dolly and Suzie stayed home and took care of household chores and their aging parents Tom and Gwendolyn. The older Thomases did everything possible to keep their girls lily white. They only allowed them to socialize with other whites in the neighborhood; but this was Jamaica, the rhythms and breezes were almost as warm and exotic as the men — and each of the Thomas girls had a mind of her own.

Suzie, the middle daughter, began exploring Cuba as an alternative to Jamaica. It was 1930 and Cuba's economy was booming. Suzie learned that money was to be made there as a hotel or casino worker.

"Besides," she told her mother, "the Americans are flocking to Cuba in droves, opening luxury hotels, restaurants and other service businesses. America has just put in place some kind of prohibition law, and I've read that many of their wealthiest now see Cuba as the Riviera of the Caribbean."

While this was being contemplated, a sheer coincidence took place. Aunt Suzie went cavorting at a cocktail party held in the home of David Chung, one of the island's wealthiest Chinese fabric merchants. Chung was well known for hosting lavish parties. He introduced Suzie to Reuben Sanchez, the overseer of a large sugarcane plantation in Cuba. Reuben was visiting Jamaica with his manager on business.

Aunt Suzie arrived home from the party beaming and blushing, "Mum, I met this great guy from Cuba. He's the most handsome and sensitive man ever created. He has jet-black, shoulder-length hair, beautiful olive skin, and emerald green eyes," she swooned. Then she let out a long sigh and moaned, "I think it was love at first sight. He is just absolutely gorgeous. He's like an Adonis!'"

"Bloody hell, just when I thought I'd succeeded in convincing her to stay with the family in Jamaica, she goes and meets a 'groovy Cuban,'" said Great Grandmother Gwendolyn as she rolled her eyes and muttered to her husband, "Tom, I think we're about to lose that girl!"

After six months of trips to and from Cuba to see Reuben, Great Aunt Suzie came home boasting a diamond engagement ring and one huge beam in her eyes. From there things progressed into frantic wedding plans, followed by a lovely wedding at the Courtleigh Manor Hotel in Kingston. An entire contingency of people who spoke no English arrived from Cuba for the festivities. Reuben's father and his boss, much to the embarrassment of the Thomases, paid for the wedding; but still struggling to make ends meet, they continued to pretend to be one of Kingston's elite families.

Great Aunt Suzie joined her new husband in Havana shortly after the wedding, and the family gave her a most mournful farewell. Over 10 years later, she delivered her third son. Her parents were about to board a boat over to Havana to meet their new grandson, when Fidel Castro and his contingency of freedom fighters arrived in Cuba. Castro started and won the revolution, and no visitors were allowed in or out of the island. The family in Jamaica never saw Aunt Suzie and her

boys again. After escaping the restrictive grips
of her parents, she ironically fell into the even
more controlling regime of communism. My great
grandparents went to their graves mourning the
"loss" of Aunt Suzie and their four grandsons.

Violet and Dolly, the sisters left behind, were
growing restless and tired of the controlled
lifestyle demanded by their parents, who refused to
assimilate into island living. Dolly was the first to
break loose with the ultimate defiance.

"I've been secretly meeting Keith Howell. You
know him. He works in Uncle Eric's shop!" she
whispered eagerly to Violet one night.

"Mum will kill you if she finds out you're
sneaking around with a Jamaican Negro," Violet
frantically whispered.

"I don't give a damn, and you'd better not be the
one to tell her," Dolly responded with arrogance
and urgency. "Promise me you'll keep your mouth
shut, Vie!"

"You're not having sex with him, are you?" Violet
responded with genuine concern. "Tell me that
you're not having sex with him, Dolly Thomas!"

"Not yet, but I sure would like a good bashing
from him," Dolly whispered mischievously. "He
looks like a six-foot tall, muscular Mandingo
warrior with the most beautifully defined arms and
chest I've ever seen. I want him Vie, and I mean
really badly. Every time I lay my eyes on him, I feel

a real warm tingle in my loins."

Six months later, Aunt Doll had even more to report, but this time the news was for her parents. She proudly announced that she was "with child," and that the father is the big, black "Mandingo warrior" look-alike from Uncle Eric's shop. The family retreated in shame for the next six months. They allowed no visitors, trying to keep "that damn Dolly's" pregnancy a secret. And all attempts by her to contact the man who had fathered her child were rejected by the older Thomases.

Dolly's son screamed his way into the world with the help of a local midwife. He was immediately given to the Mandingo's family to be raised. Dolly, distraught, was ordered to keep her mouth shut or be disowned by the family. She was too timid to challenge her parents. And after delivering a child, Dolly was even more vulnerable. After that, she never saw her son until he was almost 10 years old.

Two years later history repeated itself. Violet announced that she was also pregnant by another Jamaican.

"Dolly, I will NOT be giving up my baby and neither do I intend to leave the family home," she swore in secret to her sister one hot August evening. "What they did to you and your son, I will not let them do that to me. I will fight for my baby," she continued now very defiant. "I work and contribute to this household. No one, I mean no one, is going to throw me or my child out of this house."

"But Vie, how are you going to get Mum and Dad to agree with this?" Dolly asked, startled by her sister's resolve.

"Mum and Dad are now up there in age, and they need the money I bring in. I'll fight them tooth and nail 'till I get my way!"

Violet had been working as shopkeeper for a nearby Chinese merchant. She had become very valuable to her employer, and she had even learned to speak fluent Chinese. She worked right up until the first labor pains brought her to her knees.

Miss Birdie was born to Violet Thomas and Clinton Cole on March 3. Clinton Cole was allowed nowhere near the house to see his child; but Violet remained vigilant. She fought all resistance efforts from the family. And years later, Violet became head of the household. She provided most of the finances needed to care for her aging parents, while Dolly stayed home to give the physical care they needed.

As a child I watched my mother run both her own household and what had now become Violet's household. Miss Birdie single-handedly buried grand uncles Eric and Patrick, Grand Aunt Doll and Grandma Violet. None of them had married or raised families of their own. She buried each of them in the cemetery by the sea at Port Royal, a peninsula outside of Kingston; but one nagging question stayed with the family. Where were Aunt

Suzie and her boys? Did they survive the revolution? What was their life like in Cuba?

chapter 8

Mass Pet and Miss Birdie

TALL, STRONG AND HANDSOME — THOSE words described the man Aunt Doll's son Kenrick had become as he grew into manhood. His father's family raised him in poverty; yet he was a well-mannered and hard-working young man. At 19 years old, he began clerking at West Indies Sugar Company in Clarendon (also called WISCO). It was almost impossible to find work in Kingston, so Kenrick reluctantly resorted to life in the country.

Standing at six-feet, two-inches tall with curly brown hair, smooth olive skin, and his mother's baby blue eyes, Kenrick, aka Ken, was quite the ladies' man. "Darling, every time I lay my eyes on you I'm haunted by this deep longing in my heart" is the line he used to win the attention of his latest love interest, a girl who just happened to be his boss' most treasured daughter. Few women could resist those baby-blue eyes staring adoringly at them from that exotic brown face. Ken quickly joined the local cricket and soccer clubs in nearby Lionel Town. Between chasing women and partying, he was one hell of an athlete. Of course, the extent of his athletic prowess depended on the number of 180-proof rums he consumed with the boys the night before.

You could also find working at WISCO and getting their fair share of the local women's attention, Mass Pet and his best friend Rough Scully. These two also kicked up their own dust on the cricket and soccer fields. Pet, Rough and Ken soon became known as the "terrible three" of the entire area between Portland Cottage and May Pen. Their favorite pastime was relentlessly sowing their wild oats. On Friday evenings, Mass Pet would strum his guitar in Portland Cottage's town square. He savored the looks on the women's faces, as they swooned and wished that they could have him all to themselves. Rough and Ken would be busy working the crowd, declaring "that's my best friend." They figured this declaration and claim might help get them a bigger share of notoriety and female attention. Not that they needed it, with their handsome selves as perfectly attractive sales tools; but when the testosterone was running high, there was just no stopping them.

One of those swooning women was my sister Dahlia's mother, Annie. She announced that she was pregnant during her liaison with Sedith's youngest son. Mass Pet's future father-in-law was a local shopkeeper with a mean grin, Bruce Barclay. The couple married, and Dahlia made her grand entrance into the world soon after. By the time she was a year-and-a-half old, the two divorced. And you guessed it — Sedith played a big role in the split. She also took Dahlia in at Twickenham, so she could "raise the child to be a true Jennings."

One evening after an exhausting soccer game and over a bottle of Guinness stout at the local rum bar, Ken and Mass Pet began reminiscing about his short stint as "Mista Barklay's son-in-law." Ken said to his friend, "Pet, what the hell were you thinking? There is no way on God's earth that either your mother or that cantankerous Bruce Barclay would have allowed any kind of marriage between you and Annie to last."

"Ken me boy you are absolutely right," Mass Pet sighed and responded. "But how the hell was I to figure all that out at the tender age of 22? I was having a great time sowing me wild oats and ended up falling in love. What the hell, you live and you learn. I'll tell you one thing though. The next time I decide to make another swooning young thing happy, I plan to be a lot more cautious about that thing called love."

"You're full of shit!" Ken laughed, looked at him endearingly and declared, "You'll start quivering over some young 'filly,' and the next thing I know you'll again be trying to swim upstream without a paddle. Do me a favor, next time make sure her daddy is a little less mean, will you old boy? I don't think me nerves can take the drama a second time around."

"And here I thought you were my best friend," Mass Pet grinned and commented mischievously. "Do I need enemies with friends like you?"

"Anyway, you old playboy, my cousin Birdie Thomas is coming to visit me next week," Ken said less playful now. "I want you to stay away from her Pet — I'm not joking. She is a tough cookie from the city, married to a gambling Chinese husband. The poor girl has two young sons and that husband of hers gambles away his paycheck before payday every week. Poor Birdie works morning, noon and night on her sewing machine making clothes for the neighborhood women and men. This is how she supports her boys. She's coming here to get away from her troubles, and I don't want you anywhere near her with your womanizing self and charming lyrics."

Mass Pet listened intently and replied, "Hey, you know the girls can't resist my gorgeous backside. I'll try to contain myself even if she begs me for a piece of this irresistible loveliness."

"I'm warning you Pet, stay away! I don't need you

humping her, and me having to listen to her bawling more tears on my shoulders after you move on to your next victim. She has enough problems with that damn, no-good, husband of hers. Promise me that you'll lay off, you old bastard!" Ken cursed and pleaded.

But the more Ken carried on about his cousin, the more curious Mass Pet became. He couldn't help but think she must be one special woman for Ken to be so protective and worried.

A week later Miss Birdie arrived, and as a true city girl, this was her first trip to the country. Mass Pet later described his first "sighting of the woman" with a huge grin and a beam in his eyes. "Miss Olivia, I felt like I was hit by a thunderbolt of gorgeousness!" Then he continued, and I could see the love and excitement coming through. "She had the face and body of a goddess — the smallest waistline I'd ever seen. And hips and legs designed to drive a man to drink white rum 'till he tumbles down."

"Her face was as beautiful as a brown-skinned Cleopatra, and when she walked by in those high heels I had to chastise myself, 'Pet, stay away from her and for God's sake, keep your draws up before Kenrick murders you with his bare hands!'"

Just as I began roaring with laughter he continued, "Then she approached me with hips swinging as she crooned in her city slang, 'So you are the infamous Pet Jennings!'"

"Well, Miss Olivia, it was all over. I was now debating, 'Boy, Ken goin' have to kill me, but I got to have her, by the hook or the crook!'"

"What do you mean, Papa?" I'd respond, egging him on.

His eyes were now on high beam. "Miss Olivia, I had both of me hands out in front of me face, looking from the left hand to the right hand, whispering, 'Ken … gorgeous city creature.' Then I repeated the options a few more times, again looking from me left hand to me right hand, chanting, 'Ken … Birdie Thomas with the killer body.' All of a sudden, I felt like a damn Tasmanian Devil was perched on me right shoulder, whispering in me ear, 'If you mess with me, I going to stick me fork right in your neck!'"

"Then what happened, Papa?" I continued to taunt him.

"I must have made the right choice, because here you are years later, bringing fatherly pleasure into me life." He replied, bigger twinkle in his eyes.

But Miss Birdie's story was a little different. According to her, Cousin Ken was secretly warning her: "Stay away from Pet Jennings. If you think your no-good husband is giving you grief, Pet Jennings will rip your heart out of your chest! He has had his share of women in town, and if you drop your draws for him, don't come crying to me."

"Miss Olivia, I was innocently escaping from

the stresses of Kingston life, and in walked your father with muscles like Mr. Jamaica and shoulder-length black hair." She continued. "He was the most handsome Coolie (Jamaican slang for Indian) man I'd blessed my eyes on. I realized that if I didn't heed Ken's warning and ended up getting me heart ripped out of me chest, I would be on me own. And I kept thinking, I just put me husband out — all I need now is a heartbreaking country 'gigolo' to finish me off completely."

Miss Birdie continued, now with pure mischief in her eyes, "But when he answered, 'Yes, I'm the infamous Pet Jennings and woman ... you are a goddess,' it was all over."

The two soon became an item in Portland Cottage, with a whole lot of gossip among the local girls. Whispers about how horrifying it was for Pet to "take up," not only with a city woman; but with a married one at that — and, "Child, she also has two pickneys (Patois version of pickaninnies or children)." The more they gossiped and whispered, the more fun Miss Birdie, "the town gal" was having flaunting her fine mulatto behind around with the most gorgeous Coolie man to be found anywhere near Portland Cottage.

Sedith caught wind of this and threw as big a tantrum as any religious matriarch could afford without ruining her God-fearing image. When Mass Pet blew her off, she resorted to praying and psalm reading. Since Sedith was the major financier of the Adventist Church, she now had the preacher and the congregation pleading with the Lord that her son sees the "evil of his ways and stops gallivanting around town with that wanton, married city woman."

What were the results of Sedith's praying and tantrums? After one of Miss Birdie's returns to Kingston, Mass Pet decided to take things into his own hands. He announced to his friend Rough Scully, "You and me going on a trip to Kingston, and I don't want to hear one word out of you mouth."

Before Rough could figure out what the hell was going on, his friend had borrowed one of WISCO's trucks, and they were both "burning tires" to Kingston. They pulled up in front of Miss Birdie's house and Mass Pet yelled, "Birdie, I come to rescue you. Let us get moving before that no-good husband of yours shows up and I have to choke him!"

The two men quickly packed her belongings, including Miss Birdie's two boys, into the truck and headed back to Mass Pet's small cottage in Lionel Town, Clarendon. He soon helped mastermind her divorce, they married, and two years later I was born. Another two years later my brother Clinton screamed his way into the world.

Some of my fondest memories of Mass Pet were "deliciously awful." He'd walk with me in his arms through the most beautiful tropical fruit trees in our backyard, pointing at them and saying, "This is mango, this is pomegranate, this is sweetsop ..." and then he would pick the ripest, most succulent sweetsop, break it open, take the seeds out, and let me bury my face into the fruit as I slurped and devoured it. After we both had a bellyful, he would put my face under the garden hose so Miss Birdie wouldn't have to yell, "What you do with the poor pickney? She has food all into her nose. Pet, what is wrong with you?" This was a "delicious" memory.

Then the following evening I would run frantically and hide under the bed as Mass Pet roared home from work on the loudest, biggest triumph motorcycle I'd ever had the displeasure to seeing or hearing. He'd scare me half to death, and I'd take cover until he turned the motor off. Then he'd trudge through the house yelling, "Miss Olivia, I turned the monster off, so you can come out of hiding and jump into me arms for a big, old smooch!" This was an "awful" memory of Mass Pet.

Other memories of my delightful father include sitting under a poinciana tree at night under a full Caribbean moon, eating coconuts sprinkled with brown sugar and sipping lemonade from an aluminum cup. Mass Pet would be strumming his guitar and singing, "Brown skin gal, stay home and mind baby..." as he winked at Miss Birdie, who looked on adoringly. Even as a child I recognized an intense love between them; but I also thought

Miss Birdie's love for him bordered on obsession. I'd overhear her telling her best friend that he was womanizing again. The friend would advise, "Lord Birdie, what you complaining about? As long as he takes care of you and the pickneys, you should make that bounce off of you back."

But Miss Birdie was not the type of woman to turn the other cheek, and she raised lots of hell at any suspicion. She also got jealous if she thought he was spending too much time with his own children. She spent a lifetime wanting her husband all to herself; but he was well loved by all, a suspected womanizer, and he had an incredible adventurous and free spirit. When he began his work stints in Europe, Miss Birdie followed him to far-off lands out of fear and insecurity and to keep an eye on things. She really wasn't satisfying any adventurous yearnings of her own. I watched and hoped that my own relationships with men would be more trusting and less torrid; but oh, how I loved and admired them!

chapter 9

Letters From Cuba

*L*IKE DARK CLOUDS OF MYSTERY AND unease, Cuba brought conflict, mayhem, anarchy and murder to our family. We were geographical neighbors, but the strife experienced by one island far surpassed anything ever endured by the other.

It was the 1950s and Great Aunt Suzie had been living in Cuba for over 10 years with her husband Reuben Sanchez. Sanchez was the overseer of a sugarcane plantation in Santa Clara in the province of Oriente. Spanish descendant Ernesto Revuelta owned the plantation. Aunt Suzie had given birth to four sons Juan, Reuben Jr., Patrick and Luis. She kept the family in Jamaica informed with long letters about Cuba, its people, its volatile political upheavals, her challenges with learning Spanish, and her life as Mrs. Reuben Sanchez.

Aunt Suzie wrote that Cuba had become a plantation aristocracy, with a financially strong upper class and a huge lower class of poor, mostly black Cubans. These blacks were descendants of a lucrative and active slave trade. After slavery was abolished in the United States, many American plantation owners moved to the island nation. Its abundance of slaves made this a very good move for the Americans, who now had an ample supply of black labor to keep the plantations profitable.

Mass Pet was now our storyteller. Unlike Sedith's tales, his stories unfolded live, right before our eyes. He told us that Cuba now provided much prosperity for the land-owning descendants of Spaniards or Criollos, who had slowly moved into the island in abundance during the past several centuries. So Reuben's employers, the Revuelta family, enjoyed all that the sugar-rich island had to offer.

Great Aunt Suzie wrote in her letters that they hosted opulent parties, where guests ate fine food and enjoyed an abundance of expensive liquor and cigars. She worked as hostess at many of these swanky affairs. In one letter she lamented that, had she not already built a life with Reuben, she would have actively sought to marry one of the wealthy Criollos. After all, she was a beautiful blue-eyed Brit who would have no problem snagging one of the Spaniards. And my great grandparents, in all their wisdom, were quick to comment, "If Suzie had to end up in Cuba, she should not have been in such a rush to marry Sanchez. After all," they proclaimed, "if she had married one of those wealthy Spaniards the entire Thomas family may have moved to Cuba. Some of that wealth and prosperity could have been made available to us."

Why their three beautiful, blue-eyed daughters had to end up with men of color in both Jamaica and Cuba was baffling to the older Brits.

"Where did we go wrong?" asked Great Grandmother Gwendolyn. "Maybe if we never migrated to the islands, we would have been able to keep our family tree untainted, just like it was in the earlier days," she sighed.

The Revuelta family's sugarcane plantation in Cuba was vast — close to 600 acres, Aunt Suzie wrote. Centuries earlier, more than 300 slaves toiled to plant and harvest the crops there. There were about 80 makeshift quarters on the property. Most of them were now empty or partially deteriorated. The slaves had been cramped into these quarters during earlier years; but now local paid laborers working the plantation used them as resting places. Reuben and Great Aunt Suzie lived in a rustic two-bedroom cottage on the estate with their four young sons.

On the other hand, the Revueltas lived in a magnificent six-bedroom mansion on the estate. It was more like a palace, with vast 14-foot-high windows and an enormous wrap-around veranda surrounded by lilies, roses and bougainvilleas. Aunt Suzie described in a letter a spectacular winding staircase of imported Italian marble, which led to the master suite upstairs. And the enormous 20-foot-high entranceway to the mansion boasted the Revuelta family's Coat of Arms.

But by the 1950s, the Revueltas were struggling to maintain their opulent lifestyle. Slavery had long ended, and a significant amount of capital was needed to transition their cheap labor-based sugar enterprise into a more modern business run by machines. This capital was to come through partnerships with the Americans who had been gradually populating the island "en masse." However, this indebtedness came with demands for increased production and expense control. There were no more opulent celebrations after harvest. Life on the plantation had transitioned from extravagance to a daily exhausting grind. The Revuelta's struggle to pay their debts eventually ended when they painfully and reluctantly had to turn over the deed to their beloved estate to those thought earlier to be the "enabling Americans." After an emotionally demoralizing ritual where the Revuelta family's Coat of Arms was removed from the mansion's vast entranceway, the family was retained to run the plantation with the help of Reuben, Great Aunt Suzie and their four teenage sons.

Mass Pet read another letter from Great Aunt Suzie to us, in which she described the latest political upheavals in Cuba. "Batista has taken over power and appointed himself as the country's leader. The existing president and his cabinet went into exile, and it is now evident that Cuba's political future is about to change drastically," she wrote. "Continued resistance and mistrust of Batista's regime has resulted in a tightening of dictatorship and repression, and Cubans at all levels were feeling the 'bite.'"

There was opposition to Batista's government everywhere in Cuba, according to another letter. The loudest protests and demonstrations were coming from the island's university students. One student named Fidel Castro had captured the attention of all including the press and Batista's government. Castro was viewed as a "loose cannon." He had already participated in riots and attempts to overthrow governments in both the Dominican Republic and Columbia. He was the son of sugar planters in the nearby province of Oriente and a law student.

In support of Aunt Suzie's letters, the *Jamaica Gleaner* reported that Castro led a failed attack on an army barracks in Santiago de Cuba. He was sentenced to 15 years in prison for this; but things got even worse in 1955. *The Gleaner* reported that Batista had again inaugurated himself as president. The dictator was able to do so because of rampant absenteeism from the opposition during another makeshift election. After this triumph, Batista became so self-confident he made the mistake of freeing most political prisoners, including Fidel Castro, who reportedly fled Cuba for exile in Mexico, according to news on the radio.

Meanwhile, in the international news section of *The Gleaner*, there were more articles on the alleged organization of many Cuban exiles in Mexico. Mass Pet read to us that an infamous Argentine doctor named Che Guevara had joined these exiles. *The Gleaner* reported both open and secret activities by this group of dissidents, including military training and fundraising. There was speculation and local editorials about the dangerous intent of this group, and their reputation for stirring up political dissidence in several countries. Mass Pet and Miss Birdie discussed this "political time-bomb" and openly hoped and prayed that the dissidents came nowhere near Jamaica.

Great Aunt Suzie's letters became increasingly troublesome. She described a Cuba overtaken by American tourists and businessmen. She declared that prohibition in the United States had given way to thousands of unemployed saloon owners and workers relocating to Cuba, especially to Havana. There were also American-owned distilleries and breweries, hotels, restaurants and casinos.

Aunt Suzie wrote, "It appears that all that have been frowned upon in America have now relocated to Cuba. After all, Cuba is now being called the Riviera of the Caribbean and is often compared to exotic European locations such as Nice and Monte Carlo. Americans are flocking to the island in droves to indulge in all types of activities." Great Aunt Suzie expressed strong concerns about all of this.

In another letter she expressed with much disdain, "One of the most disturbing trends now is the opening of hundreds of whorehouses and other places of ill repute in Havana. Prostitution has become big business. Many mothers are watching their beautiful daughters succumb to the seduction of the brothel, with all its financial rewards."

Then she continued, "Of course, along with prostitution and gambling come certain less desirable elements. Havana is fast becoming a Sodom and Gomorrah. Visitors openly enjoy all the liquor, whores and pornography that they can get. Something is going to give," Great Aunt Suzie wrote, "And I have a feeling that when it does it will not only be traumatic and devastating, it will also be life-altering."

There was no communication from Great Aunt Suzie for several months after this troubling letter. My parents continued to discuss developments in Cuba that they learned from the press. Mass Pet and Miss Birdie loved to discuss politics, so they openly debated about what news may be fact and what was sensationalized.

Then in December, there were local press reports
that an expedition headed by Fidel Castro and Che
Guevara landed at Oriente province by boat from
Mexico. Great Aunt Suzie's suspicions were coming
true. The family in Jamaica began to wonder fearfully
about her fate and about what would become of her
boys. There was talk of attempting to get them out
of Cuba and back to Jamaica; but no one knew how
to accomplish this — what with all the turmoil and
uncertainty being reported by the press. The local
press reports became increasingly frightening, with
killings, strikes and another election called by Batista
that was again reportedly "rigged."

Mass Pet read to us that Castro's revolutionaries
persisted and that Batista fled into exile in the
Dominican Republic the beginning of the year
in 1959. *The Gleaner* reported that Guevara and
hundreds of revolutionaries immediately took
Havana. Batista's regime had already closed the
door on any hope for a democratic process in Cuba.

In February of 1959 the local press reported that
Castro became Cuba's Prime Minister; but after
conflicts with a new president named Urrutia, he
resigned his post in just a few months. Urrutia was
quickly removed as president and replaced with
one of Castro's political cronies, Torrado. Shortly
thereafter, Castro was again Cuba's Prime Minister.
Mass Pet commented sadly as he read to us,
"Children, this does not sound good. I think it will

be a very long time before any of us will see or hear from Great Aunt Suzie."

But miracles do happen. A letter arrived unexpectedly from Great Aunt Suzie. We'd waited 10 long months in fear without a single word; but this letter was even more daunting!

It chronicled the following: She, Sanchez and the boys were home at the plantation the night that Castro and his revolutionaries landed. She wrote, "There were sounds of helicopters hovering overhead all night. Explosions and persistent gunfire came from the east. Terrified and confused, we took cover under the tables and beds in the cottage. The unbearable terror continued all night."

She continued, "At about four in the morning, there was a gruesome silence. Half hour later, our hearts continued to pound. Reuben and my boy Patrick left the cottage armed with two shotguns and a flashlight. They moved quickly, like thieves in the night, heading to the main house. The plan was to check on Revuelta and his wife Caridad.

"An hour later, they slid back through our front door. Patrick carried a trembling, wailing and disheveled Caridad in his arms. We stared at them, stunned."

Great Aunt Suzie's letter continued: "Her eyes were red and sunken into a deep hole. She was as pale as a ghost. Her face could be likened to a frightened animal. I rushed to comfort Caridad and was stopped dead in my tracks by a bizarre emptiness in Reuben's eyes. Stuttering and gibbering, he tried to make sense as he relayed the following. He and Patrick were on their way to the main house when they saw the shadows of two bodies sprawled on the ground in front of them. The figures, one almost headless, lay eerily in front of an abandoned barn. The victims were shot in the head, and their throats were cut. Warm blood still dripped from their lifeless flesh onto the ground beneath them. In shock, Reuben and Patrick approached this spectacle. They shone their flashlights again on the bodies. Then they both recoiled in terror. They had just discovered the remains of Revuelta and his son, Carlito.

"Patrick clutched his head and yelled, 'Oh God! Oh Jesus! Where is Caridad?' Now speechless, they both ran to the main house and found Caridad on the floor in a closet. Her head was down, her arms were wrapped around her knees; she was weeping and rocking from side to side in a complete daze."

Mass Pet lowered his voice in disbelief as he read on: "Caridad, between wails and tremors, recounted. At around midnight, her husband and son hid her in a closet in Carlito's bedroom. They crouched in the living room, armed with two shotguns, waiting for whatever was coming their way. A thick cloud of darkness enveloped them. Then Caridad heard the voices of men approaching the house. They pounded on the door. There was the sound of glass crashing and splintering as they forced their way into the house. More commotion, two gunshots, punching, thuds and yelling, screams in Spanish, 'Who are you? What do you want?' Then a forceful reply, 'We are the expeditionary ... the revolution has begun ... we have come to free Cuba of Batista and supporters like you.'

"More screams and a commotion ... and a dreadful silence."

Mass Pet read on as Great Aunt Suzie's letter got even more disturbing: "Caridad then bawled, 'They killed my Ernesto and Carlito, even though they too hated Batista. I have no one now — my life is over.'"

After that letter, we intermittently picked up Cuba's Radio Rebelde late at night. Jamaica and Cuba are neighbors, separated only by miles of the Caribbean Sea. Mass Pet, who understood more Spanish than he spoke, kept us abreast of the ongoing events. The Cuban people were taking to the streets, dancing, celebrating and shouting "Viva la Revolución."

According to the news, firing squads were openly ordered to kill Batista's soldiers. Looting and mayhem ensued in Havana. Vandalism was rampant. Casinos were destroyed, parking meters were smashed, and TV studios were taken over. Anarchy and confusion pervaded. We heard Castro's voice on Radio Rebelde charismatically and passionately preaching about the evils of

Cuba's existing society. Radio Rebelde reported that Cubans were embracing Castro's leadership with excitement and enthusiasm.

Later, there were frequent local reports about the takeover of medium- and large-sized agricultural estates and other privately owned businesses in Cuba. In 1962, we heard that Castro just declared that the revolution was a socialist one. Further attempts to nationalize were aggressively pursued, with government takeover of the utility companies, mass communication and the educational system. Then we heard that hundreds of Cubans were attempting to flee to Miami. When Mass Pet heard this, he threw his hands up and declared, "I don't believe it; Cuba is headed for communism!"

Miss Birdie cried and moaned, "No, this cannot be … they are our neighbors! What will become of Aunt Suzie and the boys now?"

One year later, we got the last letter from Great Aunt Suzie. She, Reuben and three of their boys had moved into a small, cramped government-subsidized apartment in Havana. Intense grief and anxiety is what she described. Her third son Patrick had disappeared. He was attempting an escape to Miami on an inner tube, he stated in a letter left for his wife and their baby. He promised to send for them very soon.

Great Aunt Suzie also wrote, "Caridad Revuelta was put in a mental institution. The poor dear never recovered from the trauma of so violently losing her husband and only child."

She warned that we might never hear from her again. This time she was indeed correct. None of her assumed future attempts to contact us in Jamaica were successful. My great grandparents mourned her like they would the death of a child. They had "lost Suzie to communism and to a Cuban." In their infinite ignorance, they seemed unsure which was worse.

chapter 10

The Loss
of Innocence

*L*IKE UNWELCOME RELATIVES, LOSS,
trauma and abandonment descended on me once
more; but I was older now. And though I had
courageously endured them before, I wondered what
fortitude would descend from above to help me
endure them once more.

My family sent my beloved sister and friend off
to boarding school. She was 13 years old. Now on
the other end of the island in St. Ann, we were
no longer together. Sending children to boarding
school was common practice in Jamaica — and yet
another custom inherited from the British. Dahlia
left just a few years after Miss Birdie's abrupt
departure to England. In the two years following
her departure, I spent most of my quiet times
longing for the summers when Dahlia and Clinton

would return for vacation so we could romp, stir up mischief, and give Sedith "more grey hairs."

The first semester after Dahlia's departure, Sedith had me join the Brownies to allay my despondence, which turned out to be a wonderful move. I now also had a best friend named Udie, who was the "brain" of the class ahead of me, and she informally tutored me in math on weekends at Sedith's urging. She was tall, dark-skinned, athletic and the only child of Mista Mack, Sedith's caretaker at Twickenham. Udie and her parents lived in a one-room thatch hut on the property. Every morning before school, Udie's chores were to sweep the ground of the hut spotlessly clean with a straw broom, make the beds, and make sure the newspaper clippings that served as wallpaper in the hut were all neatly in place.

I replaced sibling adventures with Brownie girl troop shenanigans. My school in Portland Cottage was located on a hill overlooking Twickenham on one side and the scenic Barnswell Beach on the other side. Some of my best memories included evenings with the Brownies. We'd sit at dusk overlooking Twickenham under a huge poinciana tree. I could smell the lush, bright-red flowers that shaded us as we stared at the fascinating orange sun slowly descending into the horizon. We sang loudly together in unison, as Udie and I glanced at each other smiling, "Evening time, work is over now it's evening time, man a walk on mountain, a walk on mountain, a walk on mountainside; make we put the 'vickle' in the pot, make we walk and sing, jump and play ring ding, 'cause it's evening time."

Miss Birdie sent me camping gear from England; but the troops had no tents, so we would spread old blankets on the ground and sleep innocently under the stars.

It was dusk on the first day of one of our camping trips. We had spent all day exploring Puss Gully at Twickenham, shooting birds with catapults like little marksmen, and were now preparing to cook them for dinner. Brownie Mistress Miss Hilda announced in the Queen's English, "Girls, we will now build a fire from scratch, boil some potatoes, yams and dumplings, sauté the bird meat — this should give us a hearty dinner. After dinner we will make a bonfire and sing folk songs around it before retiring. How does that sound, troops?"

"That sounds good, Miss Hilda!" we responded in excited unison.

Then she broke us up into teams. Udie was on my team, and we were in charge of building the fire. Team two was to peel the potatoes and yams; team three was in charge of making cornmeal dumplings; and team four was to prepare and sauté the bird meat. We scrambled off, chattering about finding a big log which we would use to build the fire. Miss Hilda had taught us well. Cherry yelled,

"I found the perfect log ... let's get the fire going!"

We pranced around like busybodies, grabbing up pieces of wood and twigs. We piled them on top of our newfound log, sprinkled kerosene on the pile, and rubbed two twigs together for what seemed like an eternity. Soon we had a fire going. My fellow Brownie and friend Jennifer poured water into a large copper pot, and we sat around chatting and fanning the fire with thatch palms, waiting for the water to come to a boil. Stiff, stern and starched, our troop leader busily issued directions, "Yvonne, don't stop fanning that fire. Sheryl, make sure you get all the skin off of that piece of potato without cutting yourself. We don't want to have to apply any first aid during this trip!"

It was sundown; the sea was calm and a beautiful turquoise blue-green. A warm, tranquil breeze hugged our little bodies. We were at the edge of a swamp across from Jackson's Bay Beach, tending to our chores like busy little bees in starched brown uniforms. Just as Miss Hilda announced, "Girls, you've done a great job. You learned to make fire from twigs, work in teams, and ..." suddenly, loud ear-piercing screams interrupted her praise. I quickly glanced around to behold Carol and Jennifer poised for a frantic sprint, with mouths wide open and nostrils flaring. Then I saw the copper pot moving eerily away with hot water and steam airborne everywhere. The pot moved in an easterly direction, and the troops and I headed frantically to the west, our hands flailing, legs distended, screaming and hollering in Patois. Miss Hilda yelled, "Rass Claat (Jamaican expletive), Alligator!" as she took off like a bat out of hell. That nasty shock was about to abruptly end this camping trip.

Between strides away from the scene, I glanced back in horror to see a huge alligator with tail on fire heading straight into the swamp. The "big log" that Cherry found sticking out of the bushes was the tail of that poor creature. No one knew it then, but the sleeping creature was awakened by the sting of an intense fire and went cantering off for dear life. Miss Hilda was definitely loosened up as she briskly led our unexpected sprint away from the scene. She nervously announced, catching her breath between steps, "Gggirls, let's come back for our camping gear tomorrow. Mr. Thomas and Keith (her husband and grown son) will accompany us this time. In the meantime, let's get the hell out of here!"

But we were not finished with animal capers. Our final camping adventure included an ugly and intimidating wild boar that terrorized our little troop, chasing us around for what seemed like forever. We rushed up into three trees and yelled across to each other, with Miss Hilda on the highest branch, "You all right? Him bite you?" Udie hollered "Olivia, you in one piece?" I shot back frantically, "I think so!"

The boar grew tired of waiting and disappeared before dawn, just as I was about to lose my grip on the tree branch that had become a temporary resting place. We descended and hurried home, exhausted, bodies aching and distended from the unexpected branch bed. It sure was a joy to see Cookie in Sedith's kitchen stirring a steaming pot of cornmeal porridge, with the rusty soupspoon hanging like a trophy on an iron hook over the kerosene stove. I filled my hungry belly with a bowl of steaming porridge sweetened with condensed milk, vanilla and nutmeg. Then I jumped into bed for some well-deserved rest.

More adventures were coming. A week later Dahlia, Clinton and my other brother Lancie arrived for summer holidays. Uncle Bugs expressed worries that the "town bways" (city boys) had returned, and he had a feeling that he would be the one "getting more grey hairs than the perpetual white-rum drinking" was giving him. I grabbed onto Dahlia's frock, enthusiastically telling her that while she was gone I had to have Mista Mack's daughter Udie teach me more punching and ripping skills, and that she sometimes helped rescue me from a bully she thought may be too much for me. I still had to fight my way home from school. After all, my athletic big sister was no longer around to defend me. After she left for boarding school some of my cantankerous schoolmates tried to terrorize me on the trek home.

They retaliated for the "back-siding" Dahlia used to give them earlier when they messed with me. Now I was the one putting the fear of God in them, and Udie was right there with me as needed.

My only complaint was that news about my fighting would get to Sedith before I turned the final corner for home. Instead of comforting me or chastising my attackers, she would wait for me at Twickenham's gate. Hidden hands meant that she was patiently fondling the infamous leather belt in her apron pocket. So after I gave the provoking bullies one of my now famous "back-sidings," I'd prepare my hide for Sedith's belt. She insisted that I was to avoid all fights. I thought, with spirit and determination, "Ah, you win some, you lose some ... what's a feisty young girl to do?"

But Sedith and I spent real quality time together after Dahlia's departure. Some Saturday nights after church service my friend Udie dined with us around the old lady's gorgeous antique mahogany dining table. It was always adorned with a starched-white linen tablecloth from her collection. Cookie fussed and catered, grumbling that she missed having us around because of the "damn all-day church business!"

After dinner, Sedith and I walked Udie to her hut at Twickenham. Her mother Lindie and Mista Mack had lived on the property for over 20 years. We'd head out under the stars, our path lighted by a big, round tropical moon. We were always armed with thatch palms in hand to deter the mosquitoes. Udie often jumped and grabbed Sedith's frock, declaring the latest shadow to be a "duppie" (ghost). My sophisticated grandmother would respond in disgust, "Gal, stop the foolishness. There is no such thing as a 'duppie!'"

I would hold my belly laughing, while glancing gingerly behind to ensure the "duppie" was nowhere in sight.

On Sundays, Sedith took me on sojourns through Twickenham. She checked up on her fruit trees and on how Mista Mack was managing the property. She also eyeballed to see if anyone was illegally using the property to burn coal or set up thatch residences.

Sedith lifted me up and plopped me on one hip when the terrain got rough. I could feel the steady rhythm of her thin hipbone against my loins as I wrapped my tiny legs around her waist. We'd view the foundation of the old great house as she told more stories about life on the plantation under Ian Reid's regime; but the stories were less gory now. Sedith cheerfully described the great house and its beautiful antique British Colonial mahogany furniture. She boasted about the fine linens, crockery, china and exotic silverware with elephant-tusk handles that Great-Great Grandfather Reid brought back from his trips to

India. I enthusiastically recalled, "Sedith, we have some of that silverware!"

"Ah my child, you're very smart," she'd reply with a melancholy sigh. "I inherited some of that silverware and have cherished it for years. But did you notice that some of the handles are singed?"

"Yes, Sedith. How did so many of them get burned?"

She would reply, with an even bigger sigh, "There was a lot of evil around during those days, my child. Don't ever forget the stories I told to you on the veranda. People were forced to work at Twickenham under horrible conditions in those days."

"Oh yes, you said they couldn't leave the plantation even though life was so awful there."

"Those were turbulent times in Jamaica, Miss Olivia," Sedith replied, this time with a big and troubled sigh.

But I wouldn't give up with the questions until she surrendered, "Remember the stories I told you about slavery days at Twickenham? Your great grandmother said that the silverware handles were singed in that great fire, when Twickenham was burned to the ground by the Maroons."

I reflected on Sedith's stories as she toted me back to the caretaker's hut. Now my loins were really sore from the perpetual rub of her hipbone.

Mista Mack's hut sat on the most beautiful four-acre tract of Twickenham, directly in front of an enchanting clay pond. The water was crystal clear, and a contingent of colorful tropical fish swam lazily around. Udie and I romped around the pond, and then scooted up the tropical fruit trees for a sweet and succulent feast. Later, with bellies bulging, we plopped down next to Sedith and Mista Mack inside, as they talked business.

I peered around curiously. The hut was a simple, one-room, thatch-roofed structure with wattle-and-daub walls and dirt floors. I wondered where that family got the idea to use old newspapers filled with headlines and pictures as wallpaper. It was truly resourceful.

Across from me were two iron beds, neatly adorned with quaint, handmade patchwork quilts. I marveled at how poor Caribbean people could make a simple, basic home look so neat, homey and absolutely charming.

Afterward Sedith and I explored more of Twickenham's terrain before heading home. We strolled up and down the scenic valley called Puss Gully. She told a story about a young girl who was attacked and raped in Puss Gully 10 years ago by a mentally ill man nicknamed "Crazy Joe." The entire village hunted him down, and with their bare hands, pounded him to death, Sedith said.

About half a mile later, we ascended out of Puss Gully to a terrain of sea grapes and almond trees. Then we began smelling the enchanting Caribbean

Sea — and suddenly there it was staring right at us like a vast, beautiful turquoise mirage. We walked onto the powdery white sand of Jackson's Bay Beach. Soon we began gathering huge, pink conch shells and waving at the occasional red, yellow and black canoe sailing by with fishermen chattering loudly. The canoes had net-loads of fish, shrimp and lobsters. They headed to Rocky Point Beach where dozens of market women waited impatiently for the day's catch.

Then Sedith and I headed back on another fascinating hunt for pieces of broken, ornate, ceramic pieces from the old plantation days. At home we admired our wares over hot Milo while savoring fresh, crisp Ovaltine biscuits. After jumping into bed, I would imagine the English and Scottish ladies in their gorgeous, long frocks, sipping tea from fine china cups and saucers made of the pieces we gathered that day. I didn't think about the cruelty of days past. Instead, I imagined myself as a beautiful grown woman on a fine, white horse, whip in hand, gorgeous leather riding boots on foot, classic felt hat on my head, riding through Twickenham to check on the help in a much more sophisticated way than Sedith and I did on foot that day.

The following summer, Clinton breezed back to Twickenham. He was more strong-willed and mischievous than ever. After one particular confrontation with Sedith, Uncle Bugs spanked him silly. The little "warrior," without shedding a single tear, exclaimed, "Oh yeah, watch me and you!"

Then a huge commotion was heard as Uncle Bugs bolted for cover, with Clinton pelting the house with rocks from the street. After the rock-hurling session ended, Dahlia and I let him into the house through a backdoor. We quietly bathed and scrubbed his little behind down and sent him to bed without dinner. After that, Uncle Bugs would only threaten him from afar, declaring, "Me no want the town boy to do damage to me, with his rock pelting." Then it was more goodbyes to my siblings and back to school.

I was heading home in peace one afternoon, thankful that the local bullies were not too restless. There she stood in the distance at Twickenham's gate, dressed to a "T" in one glamorous British suit. Miss Birdie was back! I didn't know whether to punch her or kiss her. She hugged me tightly, took me by the hand, and we walked together to Sedith's veranda. I was happy to see her. She was a stranger to me now. I was confused. I anxiously wondered what the coming years would be like with her around. Would she take me to England? Would she take me to Kingston? Would I remain in the country with Sedith? "Dear God of Parson Mitchell's spirited Saturday preaching," I prayed, "You gave me the strength of will and emotion to deal with Miss Birdie's abrupt departure, now *please* give me the courage to deal with her sudden return."

Miss Birdie dramatically announced that she was back in Jamaica for good. She told Sedith she could no longer withstand the cold English winters; but worse of all, her constant nightmares about her babies bawling for her with arms outstretched, dirty hands and clothing, were just too much for her to bear. She had given Mass Pet an ultimatum. He must return to Jamaica and be a more stable presence in his children's lives, or she was prepared to "go it alone."

"No more adventurous working stints in far-off places, Pet," she claimed she told him. "And if you go I will no longer compromise the lifestyle of my children in order to be your wife."

Sedith listened in silence, shaking her head now and then in agreement.

So here came more change and uprooting. Miss Birdie's return was almost as traumatic as her departure. She decided to move back to Kingston, "Where she was born and raised." After all she was a "city girl"... and this country life was just not for her. Besides, she needed to "toughen" me up. According to her, no longer was I to live a privileged life with Portland Cottage's land "baroness." City living would give me the coping skills I needed for life's future challenges, according to Miss Birdie. I wanted to tell her that I quickly learned those coping skills after she left to retrieve her handkerchief four years ago, but thought, "She'll figure that out on her own sometime."

So off I went to Kingston with Miss Birdie when the semester ended, and after a tearful goodbye with my dear grandmother Sedith. Miss Birdie owned a home on the east side of the city. My brothers Clinton, Lancie and Maxie lived there with our grandmother Vie when our mother was in England. The house was lovely, with a small indoor flower garden that separated living and dining rooms. The community had deteriorated significantly in the last four years Miss Birdie was away. My brothers were now tough city boys. Though they were never in trouble outside of the home, I could see where living with them would be a different ballgame. My older brother Maxie was a teenager and Lancie, my second brother, was about to enter his teenage years, and then there was my younger brother Clinton, the summer warrior of Portland Cottage.

My brothers took great joy in taunting me relentlessly about my strong Jamaican country accent; but I was tough, so I punched and swung at them when the taunting became unbearable. Maxie would simply laugh at me and make faces, and Clinton would punch back. Lancie merely held his arms in front of his face and body and let me punch away. While shielding himself, he boasted a big, beautiful grin and would say, "Come on little sister,

take as much frustrations out on me as you want ...
I can handle it."

An amazing connection formed between my
brother Lancie and me. He was a great swimmer. He
frequently jumped off the pier at nearby Rockfort
Beach with his buddies. After hours of spearfishing,
he came home with red snappers, grouper and
lobsters. Miss Birdie enjoyed cooking up the catch,
but she constantly nagged him about the "dangers
of diving off that wharf." Lancie, the infinite
comedian, sat us down to tell the most hilarious
tales. "I was swimming around under the sea when
I put on my brakes with a big screech and much
smoke. Then there he was, a six-foot-long shark.
And he was sharpening his teeth with a big iron file
just like the one Mass Pet has in his toolbox!"

We laughed hysterically, as he continued, "I
negotiated my way out from under Oscar the shark's
fins. As he snapped at me with his massive jaws, I
had to punch him in the eye before letting him see
my tail lights in the water!"

By the time Lancie finished his shark stories,
we'd be rolling on the floor, gripping our bellies to
stop the "deliciously awful" pain from our laughter.

Lancie was obviously Miss Birdie's favorite child,
and I didn't mind one bit because he also tugged
at my heartstrings. He was handsome and kind-
hearted, and he felt great affection toward me. A
product of Miss Birdie's first marriage, he was of

black, white and Chinese decent. Before Mass Pet returned from Europe, I always felt safe under my big brother Lancie's watchful eyes.

A few months after Miss Birdie's return, I had settled into school in Kingston. We were alone at home one night enjoying a raucous feather pillow fight. Suddenly, Clinton yelled, "Papa come!" And he jumped through the window onto our front yard. I followed closely behind to behold our beloved Mass Pet climbing out of a taxi, arms wide open as we jumped into them with glee. Out of the taxi came bags after bags, barrels and cartons of things that much to our delight suggested that he was home for good this time. The look in Miss Birdie's eyes when she came home to the presence of the love of her life was a joy to behold. We stayed up all night listening to more tales about his adventures in England, Scotland and Czechoslovakia, and his work as engineer on another oil rig in the Black Sea.

Soon after Mass Pet's return, Lancie graduated from high school and began clerking at Machado Tobacco Factory in Kingston. Every payday he headed home with gifts for us, the little ones. He also handed half of his paycheck over to Miss Birdie. His hilarious spearfishing tales were now replaced with stories about how he conquered the hearts of one girl after the other. We still held our bellies with laughter as he expounded on the sweet and tantalizing "lyrics" he now used to get attention from the girls. Lines like: "Your lips are like ripe cherries dipped in honey from a succulent bee." And how he, "wanted a big bite off of her Bombay mango."

When I grew up I hoped to find a man just like Lancie — someone kind, handsome, fun, and with an incredible sense of humor. One weekend, he announced that we were going on a special "mission." We headed out on a long trek through Kingston to a street corner in Trench Town. Lancie led the way, whipping us into more fits of laughter with his stories. Then all nine of us stopped dead in our tracks to behold the Wailers, a band led by young Bob Marley, belting out songs like "Lonesome Feeling" and "Trench Town Rock." We jumped into the crowd, dancing and singing along as the group took us on an amazing musical journey. Later we skipped home from the surprise outdoor concert still dancing and singing, with Lancie running off at the mouth that he thought Bob Marley and Peter Tosh from the reggae group were heading for "big-time" stardom. Little did we know how successful Marley was about to become.

Mass Pet faced challenges and obstacles as he tried to adjust to life back in Jamaica. Finding a job in his field that paid anywhere near what he made in Europe was difficult. And he was resistant to settling for some "bureaucratic job with the local government that paid a mere pittance." Miss Birdie stayed close to him, out of love, but more so out of fear that his adventurous instincts may take over and Europe would come calling once again.

During these struggles, Mass Pet came up with a plan to get Twickenham going again as a fully functional sugarcane farm. After all, he knew the business well, having worked for WISCO for many years as a young man. He did his research and was positioned to receive funding from the government to get the business started; but his sister Sybil intervened. Aunt Sybil voiced strong opposition to any redevelopment of the family land. She was, of course, Sedith's favorite child, executor to her mother's will, and she strongly influenced the old lady's decisions. Before long, Miss Birdie was angrily alleging that, "Sybil threw your father off the family land!"

Mass Pet became so agitated that he lashed out in anger at both his mother and only sister. I learned then that Miss Birdie had an "axe to grind" with both Sedith and Aunt Sybil. She claimed that, "They never fully accepted me as Pet's wife. They always thought that I was not good enough for him. No one was good enough for Pet in their eyes!"

While there was some truth to that, the overriding issue was Aunt Sybil's jealousy. After all, Mass Pet was the only one who gave Sedith grandchildren. She feared only her brother's children would inherit Twickenham. As it turned out, her fears would come to fruition. After all this family conflict and drama, Mass Pet took a job as chief engineer with a large Japanese-owned fabric manufacturing company recently relocated to the island. Unfortunately, the relationship between Mass Pet and his sister was never the same, and this would come back to haunt us later on.

Soon I got a scholarship from the government to attend high school at no charge. High school was a privilege not an entitlement on the island, and one could only attend for free after successfully passing rigorous academic examinations offered by the government. Unsuccessful students could only attend high school if their parents could afford to pay the tuition. Others would go to trade school or work as store clerks or laborers.

I was nine years old and attending Excelsior High School in Kingston. The school was wonderful, with a diverse contingent of teachers from Jamaica, India, England, Ireland and other parts of the world. Unlike some of the schools attended by children of more privileged families, Excelsior had students from middle- and lower-income families, who thumbed their noses at the single-sex, uppity boy's and girl's schools in the area. There were strong high school soccer and netball teams, and during annual sports competitions life was filled with fun, laughter and revelry.

But one day, terror and disgust almost got the

best of me. I had become a skilled dancer and key member of the gymnastics team. Many hours after class were spent at gym practice. One evening my good friend Donna and I were heading home after rehearsals. As usual, we were in the back of the bus, stretched out on the seats, as we rested our aching muscles. I glanced around at a very strange-looking man with bloodshot eyes staring at us. I ignored him and continued chatting with Donna about the day's activities. We got off the bus at its final stop and headed uphill together at a spirited pace; but the evening now enveloped us with an eerie cloud of darkness. "Oh no," I thought, "The streetlights are out again." There was only dim illumination from the stars above.

I suddenly picked the pace up to a swift trot, with Donna hurrying right up against me. Someone was following close behind us, and he was gaining ground. Fear overcame me, and I started humming a song by the Wailers as I frantically hightailed it, with Donna keeping pace. "Oh what the people may say ... have you ever had a lonesome feeling," I hummed.

A pair of crusty hands suddenly grabbed me by the neck from behind. My books flew into the air as I struggled to free myself from his disgusting grip. I heard my books crashing down onto the asphalt behind me. Then I caught sight of Donna frenziedly sprinting away, leaving me at the mercy of my attacker. I bawled out her name over and over. "Donna! Donna! Donna!" I kicked, screamed, clawed and punched. I was suddenly down on the ground in an empty, wooded lot close to Donna's house. Something sharp was against my throat. "My God!" I thought, "It's a knife. I'm dead!"

"Shut you mouth, or I'll kill you!" my assailant grunted.

I kept screaming. He ripped my skirt off and lunged on top of me. Then a miracle happened.

"What the 'blood claat a gwan' here (Patois expletive for 'what the fuck is going on here')?" a voice yelled, almost on top of us.

"Jeesus, it's Lancie's sister," another voice howled. "Let's kill him, now!"

My attacker jumped up and bolted.

Then I heard, "Olivia, it's Mark and Everton, Lancie's friends."

The two boys picked my trembling, half-naked body up from the dust. They both carried me home, weeping, like a baby in distress. I was ashamed and in shock. I begged them not to tell my parents or brothers. I promised I would tell the family myself. Sobbing quietly, I crept inside and stood trembling under the shower as I scrubbed my body with germicidal carbolic soap. I was overcome with revulsion. My skin burned and ached. I crawled into bed and passed out.

I was shaken awake by a loud, urgent knock on the

iron gate of our home. I glanced at the clock. It was
5:30 in the morning. I peered through the jalousie
window to see Donna's mother and father in the
feeble morning light. They stood there, wide-eyed and
terrified. They asked Miss Birdie if I was alive. They
told her Donna had bolted home in fear. She did not
tell them about the attack 'till early that morning.

My family was mortified and angry. They crashed
through my bedroom door with a barrage of
questions. "Did he rape you? Did he cut you? Did
you recognize him? Are you OK?"

I assured them that I had not been raped. I asked
to be left alone until after the police report was
done, and I was able to explain in more detail.

During my alone time, intense fear and confusion
haunted my thoughts. I prayed aloud, trembling and
agonizing. Sheer disgust and violation overcame
me. How could a man attack an innocent young
child like this? Was I dressed too skimpily? No, I
was in my modest school uniform with the starched
pleats. Did I look at him invitingly? No, I could
hardly stand to look at his horrible red eyes, and
I was sickened by his stare. What could I possibly
have done to cause this violent attack? In the end, it
was my caring brother Lancie who helped me cope.
"Olivia," he lovingly coaxed, "you did nothing to
cause this. Stop trying to blame yourself. The man
is a sick monster who just couldn't control himself.
No worries, my sister, I'm here to make sure nothing

like this ever happens to you again."

After the ordeal, my brothers met me every
evening at the bus station and walked me home.
My parents forbade me from any future friendship
with Donna Martin. It was easy — I was deeply
disturbed by that level of selfish fear that
completely negated any concern that a friend's life
may have been at stake.

Miss Birdie had now found her niche as a designer
of men's clothing. Christmas was fast approaching,
and she was glued to her sewing machine. It was
the busiest and most lucrative time for her business.
Men came from near and far as Miss Birdie whipped
out her tape measure and notebook to record
measurements and discuss Christmas fashion.
The popular trend that year was white shirts with
vertical rows of frills down the front. The locals
lovingly called them "frill-front shirts."

On December 4th, I listened with amusement
as Lancie described to Miss Birdie the glamorous
white-frill-front shirt he wanted to wear to a
Christmas Eve party. The shirt should have black
edging on each frill. He also wanted her to make
a tight pair of black pants to complete the outfit.
With his usual warm humor, Lancie joked that the
girls would, "Bawl when they behold my gorgeous
behind in this sexy outfit!"

We giggled and joked about how he wanted the
pants to hug his "tight young backside." I joined the

fun and revelry, along with our parents and brothers Clinton and Maxie. I taunted and teased, "Those pants will have to be really small to be able to hug your skinny backside. And what you mean by the girls 'bawling when they behold your gorgeous behind?' I thought I was your only girl!"

"My sister, you've been my only girl for so many years, and now you're my favorite girl! *Please* tell me you believe that, or I won't have any peace."

"The only peace my brother wants is a piece of Claudia Maxwell's 'Bombay Mango,'" Maxie joked. "Every time he sets eyes on her, his nose flares with desire." I really enjoyed this loving bantering with the family, especially when it was around my big brother Lancie.

"Boy, you better make sure you don't get some poor young girl pregnant," Miss Birdie warned. "Are you using protection like your father told you to?"

"Mama, how come you don't have that kind of talk with me?" I asked. Miss Birdie didn't have a chance to respond before my big brother jumped in.

"What? Girl, you better keep yourself quiet and don't let me have to thump and choke some unsuspecting young boy," Lancie warned. "I am your protector, remember? There will be no hanky-panky with you as long as I'm alive."

Then he held one hand out as he straddled his motorcycle and declared: "See my sister, I always have this little photo of you in my shirt pocket when

I leave home. It reminds me who the girl in my life really is."

Then he put the photo in his pocket and rode off. I watched lovingly, with a big smile on my face, as Lancie and his motorbike disappeared into the sunset — that was the last time I ever saw my brother.

I imagine Lancie breezily driving along — his head full of thoughts of the night to come — with a smile on his face, riding that motorbike in peace. I like to think he was happy. The night air is thick and humid, with a cool ocean breeze blowing, and the rumbling of the motor breaking the silence of the road. It was dark and quiet except for his engine. Maybe Lancie the angel is humming, and he knows when to go. So he leaves oh so quietly, lifting and dodging what is to come, watching painlessly from above.

And ... suddenly out of nowhere it came — a Jeep speeding along — and it was over just that fast! The Jeep with its oblivious driver sped out of a popular bar without yielding. Not even a blink of recognition that they had just collided with Lancie's motorbike. No realization that they had hit his motorbike from the side, sending his body reeling under the car where his head was stuck under the Jeep's chassis. I can barely think of this scene without crying. The Jeep was driven by two policemen, who were completely drunk and attempting to get home, and Lancie's body was dragged for several minutes before another driver frantically flagged down the drunkards, yelling that someone's head was under their Jeep.

Two policemen knocked urgently at the gate of our home. Mass Pet was in the shower. Maxie and Clinton had just left on foot to visit a friend nearby. Miss Birdie and I walked tentatively to the gate. She was perplexed. Her face was fraught with anticipation — fear was beginning to creep into her expression. I stood there. My breath stopped. Something began to crawl up inside of me, as time seemed to come to a stop ... the men talking; their words in an imperceptible foreign language; something horrible being said; something I can hear, but I can't understand. I am standing there. Time stops. And then it all rushes in as the bearers of bad news say their piece.

Miss Birdie let out a terrifying scream. It sank in. I felt an enormous need to wretch and vomit. I felt sickened and shocked. I attempted to vomit, but nothing except pain. Mass Pet came running out of the house, and they both drove behind the police car to the nearby hospital where Lancie layed broken and unconscious.

They got home early the next morning. Head down, Miss Birdie was dazed, trembling and hysterical. She clutched Lancie's bloody and tattered shirt and shorts to her bosom. She muttered, "Lancie never regained consciousness. I couldn't even say goodbye. My beautiful son is gone ... taken from me by two drunken bastards."

I was a young teenager and the devastation and loss brought me to my knees. The small picture of me was found in Lancie's shirt pocket. Now it was bloody. I silently wished I had died with him. Miss Birdie remained glued to her sewing machine for the next two days and nights. She made Lancie's white-frill-front shirt with the black edging. She also made the snug black pants to hug his "tight young behind."

We buried Lancie in the outfit that he designed. Miss Birdie did not shed a single tear at the funeral. Instead, she belted out hymn after hymn with her huge, operatic voice. She swayed from side to side, clutching Lancie's father's shoulder on one side and Mass Pet's waist on the other.

Miss Birdie was never the same after the loss of our beloved Lancie. Mass Pet put us all on notice for the next several months to listen for any sound of the front door opening late at night. Miss Birdie was leaving the house to wander the streets, hands clenched behind her hips, face in a devastating daze. She remained in shock for about six months. We walked behind her in the haze of the street lamps, begging, coaxing and pleading until she allowed us to lead her back into the house. Then Mass Pet made her hot tea, and he held and rocked her back to sleep.

The case was tried in court. Then our family went from devastation to anger. The two policemen got away with only a few slaps on the wrist. Police corruption was common on the island at the time. Our family was now one of the unfortunate victims.

I bewildered my parents by insisting on moving into Lancie's bedroom shortly after we buried him; but after much resistance they agreed. I was studying for the Cambridge O'Level examinations at the time. All students were required to pass these examinations after five years of high school or they couldn't graduate. This was another great custom we inherited from the British. Jamaican students usually left high school well prepared to attend any university abroad. Concerned about my mental state, Miss Birdie and Mass Pet openly wondered whether I could withstand the rigors of examinations while coping with the devastation we were all experiencing.

One night during studies I struggled to remain focused. I must have turned the lights out at around 2:00 a.m. About to fall into a deep sleep, I clearly heard one of Lancie's mischievous laughs. It was just like the ones he belted out when we were horsing around. I saw him enter the bedroom and sit on his favorite rocking chair in front of the bed.

"My brother we miss you terribly, are you in any pain?" I asked him.

"I was in terrible pain in hospital, but after

that there was nothing but peace, and the pain disappeared," he responded with a deep sigh. He rocked back and forth peacefully in the chair.

"I'm taking O'Level exams next week. I'm very nervous. We've been in great pain since you left us," I told him.

"No worries, my sister. I've been watching you, and you are going to pass all six subjects. I promise. I'll always be there to protect you," my brother and friend responded.

"I must go now," he uttered, rising slowly from the chair.

"Olivia, Olivia, wake up; who are you talking to?" Someone was yelling from the living room.

It was Miss Birdie. I jumped up from my daze and asked if I could answer that question tomorrow. I fell back into the most peaceful sleep experienced since Lancie died. Months later I learned that I passed all six subjects of the O'Level examinations. "Big brother was watching over me from above," I thought. Now I could handle grief, pain and any other challenges life brought my way. Lancie would remain in my heart and soul ... forever.

chapter 11

A Modern Day Fight for Twickenham

*T*HE FAMILY PULLED TOGETHER TO HELP Miss Birdie recover from the senseless demise of her dearest son, Lancie; but on the heels of empathy, love and grief came revenge, underhandedness and destruction. Some needed to jockey for position. Others needed to protect a legacy and loved ones. Challenges just kept hammering away at us, but we were ready for them.

I graduated from high school at age 15, still mourning the death of my beloved Lancie. After a while, my mother no longer got up at night to roam the streets in sorrow; but we knew it would be a long time before she would bellow those loud and infectious laughs of hers.

A year-and-a-half later, I was attending pre-college classes. Things seemed to be getting better.

Miss Birdie's spirits had improved significantly.
Dahlia was finishing her degree in nursing at
the University of the West Indies. She was also
preparing for a trip to Glasgow, Scotland to
complete a two-year course in midwifery. Maxie
now worked at Machado Cigarette Factory in
Kingston. Clinton, the "terror of Portland Cottage,"
was in high school.

Things were changing. Mass Pet came home from
work one day and announced that his company
had chosen him for a temporary assignment in
the United States. There were many discussions
between my parents afterwards. Then one evening
at dinner, they announced that Mass Pet would go
to Connecticut for a six-month assignment, while
Miss Birdie remained in Jamaica with the family.

By then I'd been agonizing about what to do
after pre-college. I reflected on the excitement in
my heart when family and friends came to visit
from overseas. My anticipation really got stirred
at the airport, each time that we sent them back
to the United States, Canada or England. I was
fascinated with thoughts of America, "the land of
opportunity."

"Papa, take me with you to Connecticut!"
I boldly asked.

"But child, you're hardly 17 years old!" Miss
Birdie protested, looking at me with disbelief.

I interrupted, "But Mama, there is ..."

"I'd worry to death if your Papa had to leave you alone in America when the assignment ends," Miss Birdie continued. "I won't hear of it, Olivia."

"Birdie, let the child talk, will you?" Now Mass Pet was the one interrupting.

"But Pet, how can you even entertain the idea?" Miss Birdie again interjected.

"Birdie, for God's sake, let the child express herself, please," Mass Pet insisted. Then he turned around and gave me a big wink. "Miss Olivia, why do you want to leave home and go to the States with me? Aren't you happy here?"

"I'm very happy here Papa, but to be honest there are opportunities in America that just do not exist on a small island like Jamaica!" I replied with cautious enthusiasm.

"Go on Miss Olivia. Now I'm really interested in what you have to say," Mass Pet replied. This time, he was really curious.

"I want to go to university like Dahlia did; but there are not many jobs that I could get here in Jamaica afterwards. In addition, I want to see and explore the world before I get tied down to college and a 'nine-to-five,'" I continued, happy to have the floor.

"And how do you plan to explore the world before settling into a regular job?" Papa asked, his interest now keener than ever.

"Well Papa, I was thinking that as soon as I turn

18, I could get a job as flight attendant with one of the major airlines … maybe Pan American." Now I was really enthusiastic. "I could fly home often to see the family. They give their employees passes to fly anywhere in the world!"

Now Miss Birdie was looking on with fear and disbelief. She shook her head as if to say no, but Mass Pet became even more curious.

"But Miss Olivia you have one more year before you become 18 years old. What would you do in America during that time?"

"My friend Carol now lives in New York, and she attends a school in Manhattan that accepts foreign nationals and provides them with the papers needed for student visas," I replied, ready for that question. "It's a two-year college, and you can transfer credits from there to a four-year college later on."

Mass Pet jumped up from his chair, looked my mother dead in the eyes, and said, "Birdie, I always knew it but now I am sure of it. This child is just like me. Let us help her fulfill her dreams of becoming a woman of the world. And I … I don't want to hear it!" He said this so passionately, Miss Birdie was speechless — and speechlessness was not one of my mother's strong qualities.

Two weeks later, Miss Birdie was sitting in front of her sewing machine making me some warm clothing, including a lovely fake fur coat.

"Will I need all these clothes? How cold does it

really get in New York, Mama?" I asked, sewing hems and attaching buttons by hand, as she finished each piece.

"Miss Olivia, picture walking around in the freezer of the refrigerator over there. That is how cold it gets in New York," she sighed, with worry and trepidation. Her eyes were glued to the motions of the needle on her sewing machine. I could see that she was sad. I hugged her.

Three months later, I was in New York experiencing my first snowstorm. I stepped out on the stoop of my apartment in Brooklyn in open-toe high heels wondering how the hell people lived like this. I dashed back into the apartment and attempted to relax for the rest of the day. I assumed that no one left their homes when it snowed heavily. Two hours later my instructor was on the phone ordering me to get to class. I was on a student visa and "lollygagging because of snowstorms was not allowed." So, I nervously fought snow, slush and subway to get to class and avoid any issues with immigration. Boy, were my toes freezing in those open-toe shoes. I told myself, "I've got to get a pair of boots and some woolen socks." Mass Pet was there for me on the weekends. By the time his temporary assignment ended, I assured him that I was ready to be on my own.

At 19 years old, I was a flight attendant with one of the major U.S. airlines. I worked flights to

Mexico, South America, and the Caribbean and to most U.S. cities. Dahlia and I shared an apartment in Brooklyn. She had completed midwifery school in Scotland and migrated to the United States to join me. She now worked as a registered nurse with one of Brooklyn's largest county hospitals.

We were young, adventurous, full of energy and fun-loving. Most weekends were spent traveling to exotic locations or enjoying some good, clean fun in the city. Clinton joined us after a couple of years. I had indeed become Mass Pet's child, and the world was at my feet as I traveled to far-off lands on my days off for a nominal fee. One weekend may find me lazing by the Mediterranean in the South of France. The next week I'd be dancing the night away at a club in London. My best friend and travel partner, Carmen Diaz, would coordinate days off so we could board a flight to Nice, Rome or London, whenever possible. Carmen shared a crash pad in Manhattan with three other flight attendants. We also bid on similar flight schedules each month so we could work together. While I visited Mass Pet and Miss Birdie in Jamaica, Carmen flew off to spend time with her parents in Puerto Rico.

I visited the family in Jamaica frequently and had become intimately involved in decisions being made about Twickenham and other family issues. My grandmother Sedith was now ailing. She was moved to Kingston so that Aunt Sybil could help care for her. Mass Pet and Miss Birdie bought a home in a small town in Clarendon. They partnered with Mista Mack, who now oversaw both Twickenham and Sedith's home.

During one of my many trips to Jamaica, Mass Pet pulled me aside and voiced concerns. "Miss Olivia," he said, "I've been observing a development that has me very troubled."

"What do you mean, Papa?" I asked. He had my full attention.

"You know that my sister Sybil has taken Sedith to Kingston to live with her," Mass Pet responded, eyes full of concern. "I am happy for that, because the old lady has not been well, and at her age, she needs someone to take care of her."

"I understand and this should be a good thing, shouldn't it Papa?" I responded, a little perplexed.

"It is child, however, you know that Sybil is close friends with Aubrey's wife Pearl, and I honestly do not trust those two witches," he continued. "Sybil has always been jealous of me because I'm the only one to give Sedith grandchildren. Her constant fears that Twickenham will eventually be inherited only by my children are now coming true. This thought has been eating away at her for many years, and I am becoming concerned about her alliance with Aubrey's devious and conniving city wife."

"Papa, you don't think that those two would attempt to pressure Sedith into selling our beloved Twickenham so they could share in the proceeds, do you?" Now he had my undivided attention.

"Ah my daughter, now you're getting the full picture. This is how I see it. They have nothing to lose since they have no children to share Twickenham's rich heritage with. So why not convince the old lady to let them sell the land so they can get their hands on some money?" Mass Pet replied.

"But Papa, selling Twickenham will be a horrible blow to the family's legacy and heritage. Money could never replace … " I responded, now with greater concern than ever.

"Miss Olivia, as God is my witness," Mass Pet passionately interrupted, "I will not stand by and allow those two women to destroy our family's heritage. The old lady is now getting senile, and if they do anything to influence her, I will fight them tooth and nail. I have a copy of Sedith's will in my possession. Twickenham is left to her surviving children and grandchildren, and I plan to ensure that her wishes are respected."

Mass Pet continued, now with tears in his eyes. "That land has been passed down to us through the generations. Our fore parents slaved with their blood and sweat to keep the legacy alive. I hunted food on that land to feed my mother and siblings after our father died, and we had no better means of survival. That land must remain with the family, and I'll be damned if I'll let some piss-assed Kingston witch infuse herself into family business and destroy our legacy."

"Papa, I'll be back to see you in three weeks." I hugged Mass Pet and promised. "I want you to keep an eye on things and to call me if anything changes. You and I will fight to preserve the family legacy, as God is MY witness."

Twickenham was heavy on my mind during the flight back to New York. I lovingly reflected on the sojourns Sedith and I would take through the property. The vivid-and-fascinating stories she told about the old sugarcane plantation's history played a critical role in our development and character. These memories strongly strengthened my resolve. Twickenham will stay with the family. My children and the children of my brother and sister will know exactly where we came from. This will continue to guide us through many of life's journeys.

The following month, Carmen and I were working one of the New York to Miami flights. Around mid-month crew scheduling called and advised that I would be working an earlier flight to Miami, replacing a regularly scheduled flight attendant who was out sick. I called Carmen and told her about the change. Her response was cheerful and positive as usual. "Don't worry my Jamaican friend, I'll see you on our regular flight this Thursday."

I awakened at 5:00 a.m. the next morning to the horrible news that our regularly scheduled Miami flight had crashed into the Everglades. In a panic, I called crew scheduling to find out if Carmen was indeed on the flight. Were there any survivors? Did Carmen Diaz make it out alive? But they would release no information until the next of kin were notified. On my flight back to New York, my voice shook as I announced the plane's safety features and paid public homage to the crew and passengers who lost their lives in last night's crash.

I landed in New York and rushed to the airport office. The news was devastating. Carmen did not survive when the plane dove into the Everglades. I listened with horror. It seems she survived the crash, but was among those eaten up by snakes and alligators in the vast Florida swamp. Carol, one of Carmen's roommates, was also working the flight. She was thrown onto safer ground, still strapped in her jump seat. She led surviving passengers into spirited rounds of Christmas carols as they waited for rescue teams to arrive.

I was scheduled to work another flight next morning on my day off. It was airline policy to keep the crew working immediately after a crash. This was supposed to allay post traumatic fears of flying.

What was left of Carmen's tattered body was flown to Puerto Rico for burial. After losing my beloved brother five years earlier, I knew not how

I'd survive another heart-rending loss. The airline sent those of us in mourning to grief counseling for many weeks afterwards.

My family made frantic calls inquiring about my safety. Relieved to talk with me, they were deeply saddened about my friend Carmen. Mass Pet and Miss Birdie insisted that I fly home on my next three days off so they could "feel and touch" me.

But mourning seems to come into our lives in waves. Sedith died six months later, and we gave her a grand farewell on a mound in the family's burial ground at Twickenham. Just like Mass Pet predicted, Aunt Sybil and Uncle Aubrey's wife soon approached him with papers to sign, approving the sale of Twickenham. They were insistent even though Sedith's final wish was that Twickenham remain with the family. Furious, Mass Pet and I drove to Kingston and called a meeting with both women.

"First of all Pet, I don't want you to think I'm trying to influence Sybil." Pearl started the meeting off on the wrong note. "But to be fair, neither of us has been blessed with children like you have. So we do not have your advantage, which is the opportunity to pass Twickenham onto our children."

Before Mass Pet could open his mouth, I responded with just as much arrogance. "First of all Pearl, neither my father nor I understand why you are here without Uncle Aubrey." I shot back, before Mass Pet could open his mouth. "You are not a blood relative, and your intrusion into our family business is neither appropriate, nor is it welcome."

"I'm not talking to you, you little bitch," Pearl growled. "I was addressing your father."

"Don't you dare refer to my daughter in that manner. To my knowledge the only 'bitch' here is you," Mass Pet interrupted, angry and incredulous. "Olivia is right; where is my brother Aubrey? And why do you feel the need to represent him in this family matter?"

"Pet, you know that Aubrey doesn't care what is done with Twickenham, which is the reason that I am stepping in," Pearl cautiously responded.

"Really now. Did Aubrey send you here to speak on his behalf? Last I heard from my brother, he was in total agreement with Sedith's wishes that Twickenham remains in the family," Mass Pet shot back with anger.

"No Pet, Aubrey does not know about our meeting or that Pearl is here." Aunt Sybil finally spoke.

"Then Pearl, I strongly suggest that you get the hell out of here before you really see my anger. This is Jennings family business, and I will discuss it ONLY with my sister or brother, do you understand?" Mass Pet stated slowly and deliberately.

"But Pet, I simply want to … " Pearl attempted to respond.

Mass Pet calmly interrupted, now through clenched teeth, "Go home Pearl before I throw you out." Then he turned to his sister. "Sybil, why have you allowed yourself to be influenced by that conniving woman? Sedith has been crystal clear in her resolve through the years that Twickenham should remain our strongest family tie and heritage, and that it should be passed down to our children."

"But Pet, I have no children, and ... " my aunt replied, with a look of defeat.

"I am not to blame for that," Mass Pet again calmly interrupted. "Twickenham will remain in our family whether you like it or not Sybil. Stop wasting your time listening to Aubrey's wife, or I'm afraid you will lose me as a brother."

Vengeance would come. I saw it in my aunt's face. As my father and I drove home, I told him, "Papa, this is not over. My gut tells me we will hear from Aunt Sybil again — and it will be ugly; but in the meantime, let's go home and enjoy the rest of my visit before we both get too weary to do so."

Several years later, Aunt Sybil retired, left Kingston, and moved into Sedith's house at Twickenham. Mass Pet and Miss Birdie had already built a lovely home for their own retirement on Twickenham's grounds about half a mile away from Sedith's home. I had left the airlines, married, and had three lovely children. My sister Dahlia had two girls of her own, and my brother Clinton was married with two children. My brother Maxie married his childhood sweetheart, and they had one child. We all lived in the United States, except for Mass Pet and Miss Birdie.

Not surprisingly, Aunt Sybil's move to Twickenham brought controversy, revenge and confusion to the family. On one of my trips home, Mass Pet reported that she had informally adopted one of Bert Harris' sons and had begun treating him like her own child. Harris was well known in the community as an opportunist and predator. Had Sedith been alive, neither he nor his son would be allowed anywhere near Twickenham. Disturbed by this news, I shook my head and asked, "Papa, is she getting senile? Anyone with any sense knows to stay away from Harris and his brood. How could she bring his son into Sedith's house?"

"Miss Olivia, Sedith must surely be turning over in her grave," Mass Pet chuckled. "I don't know what's wrong with my sister, but rest assured, I am keeping my eyes on things. I have made it clear to her that this land will remain in the family. She can do whatever she wants with her money, but Twickenham belongs to the Jennings clan. No ifs, ands nor buts."

Harris' son was six years old when Aunt Sybil took him in and began treating him like the son she never had. On another trip home, Mass Pet was supervising some repairs on Sedith's and now Aunt

Sybil's house. I talked at length to the contractor
about doing a complete restoration of the old house
so we could keep it as a local historical monument.
The contractor assured me he would love to have
the work, but that structurally the house could only
handle minor repairs like the one he was doing. Any
attempt to completely restore the old house would
be a waste of money. He advised that it would be
more prudent for us to tear the old house down
and rebuild it from scratch. The old foundation
had become too fragile to withstand any major
restoration.

One week later, my siblings and I flew home in a
rush. Miss Birdie was attacked at Twickenham as
she roamed the bushes picking fresh fruit for the
dinner table. Luckily, she had a machete with her to
pave her way through brush and branches. The old
lady is tough, and her attacker bolted as she yelled
and wielded the very sharp machete at him. We
were now extremely concerned about the safety of
our parents.

Ten years later I received a call that Aunt Sybil
was ailing and would not make it through the next
month. I flew home to Jamaica to see her for the last
time. Three weeks after that we were all back in
Jamaica to send Aunt Sybil off to her maker. During
a family meeting the night before the funeral, we
planned strategies to handle any situation that
may arise the next day. These included any lapses

in judgment made by our vindictive aunt. We also talked at length about Harris' older son, who had been in prison repeatedly for theft and other misdeeds and had visited his brother frequently at Sedith's home. This shocked and worried our family, whose only exposure to criminal elements was hearing about it on the news. And we suspected that Miss Birdie's attacker was either Harris' older son or one of his cronies from prison. After the family meeting, my brother Clinton and I strolled through Twickenham and discussed another potential strategy just between the two of us.

But the family's mourning of Aunt Sybil's death was abruptly interrupted. We gathered together at Portland Cottage Anglican Church just before the service began. A local teacher named Mrs. Thompson approached the family and advised us that she was the executor of Sybil Jennings' Will. She asked that we remain behind after burial for the reading of the Will. By now, our family was ready to tackle any situation. Clinton and I were even more prepared.

Mrs. Thompson read Aunt Sybil's Will aloud to a room filled with angst and anxiety. Richard's mother, who took no interest in the boy before now, was up front and center waiting for what may be coming her way through her son. And by now her son was a rude and rambunctious 16 year old who had begun acting like he was indeed Twickenham's owner.

Aunt Sybil left her share of Twickenham to me, Dahlia, and Clinton, and her money and stocks to Harris' boy Richard. She also willed all furniture in Sedith's house to Richard, except for the family's treasured mahogany dining table. After the reading of the Will, we set up a meeting with Richard and his father at Mrs. Thompson's home in nearby Rocky Point.

During this meeting, we advised Harris that he was now responsible for his 16-year-old son, and that Richard would now be living with him and not at Twickenham. After hearing this news, Richard threw a tantrum of major proportions.

"I not leaving the house," he screamed, pacing furiously around the living room in a fit of anger. "Miss Sybil promised me I could live there as long as I want to, and that is what I plan to do."

My family looked on at this tirade in utter amazement. I stood up, stared directly into the boy's father's face and growled, "There is no way in hell that we will allow this 16-year-old boy to live in our grandmother's house unsupervised."

"Miss Jennings, I will move in the house with him 'till he turns 18 years old," Harris conveniently interrupted.

"You will not be allowed to move into our grandmother's house on our family's property," Clinton responded with a threatening firmness. "You will now assume responsibility for your son so we can move on with our lives in peace. Am I making myself clear?"

"I not leaving; you can't make me leave. Miss Sybil said I could stay. You can't make me leave!" Richard yelled, continuing to pace around the room like a juvenile delinquent.

As we all left the room, I looked back to see the boy's father attempting to calm him down. Our family returned home to Twickenham, enjoyed a peaceful dinner, and then had another family meeting that night. We discussed the situation and planned our strategies to deal with all scenarios. Clinton winked at me across the table.

"I cannot believe that my sister would bring Harris and his son into our family affairs." Mass Pet was now expressing real disgust. "I'm more angry with that woman than I am grieving for her. Her actions are a slap in the face of Sedith and the Jennings family. Damn her!"

"Don't worry Papa, we will take over from here. Rest assured that no strangers of questionable character nor criminals will be allowed to live in Sedith's house," promised Clinton, putting his arms around our father's shoulder, while I held onto Mass Pet's hand. "This is our promise to you."

The family retired for the night, except for Clinton and me.

A big, round Caribbean moon lighted the way as Clinton and I strolled through Twickenham that night.

"Sis, remember when we would run through all that tall grass under a full moon and a sky full of twinkling stars, just like the ones above us tonight?" My brother reflected, pointing ahead of us.

"Yes, we were soooo innocent then," I sighed, looking at the beautiful and familiar sight ahead. "Sedith would open the backdoor and yell, 'Come back into the house children. Don't make me have to send Cookie after you with the big, old rusty soupspoon.'"

"Ah yes. Then we would pull foot like the slaves did in the old days. Only, this was an innocent and playful trot back to the old house, because we knew that Cookie had made us her delicious, steaming hot Milo with vanilla and nutmeg," Clinton lamented between more sighs. "And we would soon be slurping it down with a mouth full of Ovaltine biscuits, our little feet playfully dangling under Sedith's famous starched white linen tablecloth."

"Then Sedith would always yell, 'Don't get any of that Milo on my lovely white linen!'" I added. "And we would smile at each other because we had already made a mess. Cookie would have more scrubbing to do on the white linen tablecloth come tomorrow."

"Clinton, remember the powerful and graphic stories Sedith took the time to share with us on the veranda and under that poinciana tree over there?" I continued with an even bigger sigh. "The old lady would literally transport us back to the days of slavery. We would experience so many emotions as she moved us slowly through those stories. Anger, disgust, awe, victory — there were no limits to the feelings her amazing stories brought out in us. She even shocked us into learning about sex, right from the lips of our own grandmother! Those stories helped mold me into the woman I am today."

"Ah, Miss Olivia, those were indeed the good old days," Clinton sighed, looking up again at the beautiful moon above us. "What the hell happened that has brought us to where we are today?"

This comment jolted me back to reality, and I responded, "Don't know, my brother, but tough times call for tough measures. We will do what it takes to preserve the Jennings family legacy."

"Mass Pet and Miss Birdie are now getting up there in age, and we are all living overseas. We cannot afford to have anything resembling a criminal element nearby and certainly not in Sedith's old house. Harris' other son scares me, Miss Olivia. And after we return to the States, he may get ideas of moving his brother back into the house so he will have a place to lay low during prison breaks," said a very concerned Clinton.

"We cannot leave the island with this being anywhere near a remote possibility," I responded. I was truly afraid and continued. "Papa is too old to have to deal with this kind of problem. The thought of our father trekking through the woods at 72 years old with his shotgun to confront that type of lowlife scares me to death. The thought of Miss Birdie having to wield another machete in some criminal's face also puts the fear of God into me. We must move ahead with our secret plan no later than tomorrow night."

"You're absolutely right, Sis," Clinton shook his head in agreement. "We must do this to protect Mass Pet and Miss Birdie. We will tell Dahlia after the deed is done."

With a truck, four men, and a sense of urgency, we were up early the next day knocking loudly on Mista Mack's door. Clinton instructed him to supervise the men as they moved all furniture from Sedith's home to Richard's father's house. They were to move the family's mahogany dining table into Mass Pet's home. It would fit nicely next to his mahogany cigar-cutting table. Our father spent a lot of quality time there alone that day, rolling and cutting his cigars made from the fine tobacco he grew at Twickenham. Clinton and I spent the rest of the day planning our next move.

Then the time had come. It was now 9:00 p.m. Clinton and I moved slowly through the bushes of Twickenham to the home that had housed Sedith's family for three generations. We were like eerie shadows in the night. We both headed straight for the outdoor pantry where we found a large bottle of kerosene oil, matches, old newspapers hidden by Mista Mack, and two torches.

Clinton fired up the torch in his left hand. The resolve in his face was indisputable, as the burning torch illuminated our bodies. I held the second torch anxiously in my right hand. My brother leaned over and set it ablaze. I felt my thin body enveloped by an unsettling heat. Like phantoms in the night, we crept through the empty old house, Clinton leading the way. This time, he didn't leave me in the dust. I followed closely behind, peering through every corner and crevice. Our heavy breathing sent a sinister echo through the house. We entered the living room and carefully surveyed it. No one was there. We crept from one bedroom to the other. No one was there. Then we exited through the rear door, spun around, and quickly sprinkled kerosene at the foundation of our beloved grandmother's home. Like Maroons in an extraneous ritual, we swiftly set the house ablaze, one torch at a time.

An incredible heat overcame us. We recoiled, and then we bolted to safer ground. I spun around to behold the bright orange flames fatally engulfing the old house where Sedith nested, raised children, and told stories to her grandchildren. A single cane rocking chair swayed menacingly in the hot wind. Then it went up in flames. "Damn it!" I thought, "The men must have forgotten to put it on the truck with the rest of Sedith's things."

Then there it was, beyond flames, under the full tropical moon. It was Sedith's tombstone, standing prominently and proudly on the highest mound in the family's burial ground. I stared incredulously at that awesome sight. Clinton grabbed my hand with an unprecedented urgency — he too felt riveted by the scene.

That instant, I thought I saw Sedith looking on with a victorious and proud smile. Her smile said, in no uncertain terms, "Yes! Now the foundation of my house will be proudly displayed at Twickenham, just like the foundation of the old plantation great house. And my great grandchildren will roam the property while listening to stories about my life and the lives of our forefathers — our Maroon forefathers who fought by fire to free us from the misery of the plantation. Now you, my grandchildren, have freed us and Twickenham from the clutches of criminals and low lives. Well done, my beloved grandchildren. Now I will truly rest in peace!"

chapter 12

Democratic Socialism

$\mathscr{P}$OLITICS, IDEALISM AND SUPERPOWERS
make hostile bedfellows! And the friction can
be much more intense for a small-island nation
struggling to survive in a world led by large
capitalist societies.

By the 1930s, Jamaica had become a melting pot
of exotic racial mixes and proud blacks, with a
rich and potent cultural heritage. It had developed
a strong class structure of upper, upper-middle,
middle and lower-class citizens.

Today, many of the upper and upper-middle
classes are immigrants and their offspring who
came to the island with money and skill sets.
They are Jews, Chinese, Syrians and Portuguese,
as well as blacks, browns and East-Indians who
have also successfully climbed the social ladder

as entrepreneurs and farmers. Jamaicans of all
ethnic backgrounds now owned old plantations
like Twickenham abandoned by white people
who fled Maroon vengeance. When agriculture
failed to satisfy the needs of the population, many
Jamaicans migrated to other islands such as Cuba,
Panama and Belize to find work. Thousands also
migrated to more developed countries such as
America, Canada and England.

Hardships related to the Great Depression in
more developed countries sparked Caribbean
rebellions and fighting for people's rights in the late
1930s and 1940s. Then came the formation of the
People's National Party (PNP) in the late 1930s,
and a new opposing party called the Jamaica Labor
Party (JLP) in the early 1940s.

With the inability of agriculture to maintain
the island's economy, Jamaica became involved in
other industries in the 1950s and 1960s, to sustain
its population. Two of these primary sectors were
the mining of bauxite and tourism. Bauxite is the
base mineral used to manufacture aluminum. By the
1960s, aluminum was playing a very important role
in the world's large capitalist countries.

Jamaica's long fight for self-government came
to fruition in 1962, when the country gained full
independence from England. I remember it well,
with huge celebrations and lots of reggae and
ska rhythms. We danced in the streets for weeks.

There were independence song competitions; we selected the colors of our new flag; and we created a patriotic new national anthem that we began to sing at assembly in school. There was no more singing of Britain's "God Save The Queen." It was a time of revelry, celebration, patriotism, ethnic bonding, and a triumphant feeling that we had finally prevailed over huge obstacles.

By the 1960s, the little island of Jamaica had become the largest producer of bauxite in the entire world; but the total revenue from bauxite that remained in the Jamaican economy was minimal. The industry was entirely foreign-owned. Expatriates were brought to the island, and they lived in huge mansions with local maids, gardeners and company cars. Work in the bauxite industry paid well by Jamaican standards; but the highest paid jobs with the richest benefits went to foreign nationals. The same could be said about the tourist industry — over 50 percent of the hotels were owned by foreign companies.

Jamaica's social climate was unique and mesmerizing. Music had always been a key pulse of the island's culture with performers like Bob Marley taking Jamaica's reggae music to international levels. Jamaicans used this music to express both political and social concerns. I fondly and frequently reflected on that walk my brother Lancie took us on to jam and revel to young Bob Marley and the Wailers performing on a street corner in the ghetto. Jamaican music went from ska to rock steady to reggae. It would take over our bodies and souls like a hungry and insatiable spirit. There were no more rebellions. We expressed our frustration, love, sadness and joy through music and dance — and what a potent release this was.

The politics in Jamaica were taken over by two families of "brown" Jamaicans, the Manleys and the Bustamantes. In the 1970s, Michael Manley had emerged as Jamaica's most charismatic leader and Prime Minister. Manley was the son of another popular former Prime Minister, Norman Washington Manley. The older Manley had been the leader of the PNP for several years.

Miss Birdie and Mass Pet moved out of Kingston in 1969 to a nice home in the country, about 15 miles from Twickenham. My father continued his engineering consultancy with the Jamaican government. Miss Birdie worked on several entrepreneurial clothing design and arts-and-craft projects. They seemed happy and content — and I looked forward to a few trips per year to visit and check on their wellbeing.

After returning to the U.S. from one of my visits in 1978, there were many troubling articles in the American press about increasing political and economic challenges facing Jamaica. And this, coupled with monthly letters from Mass Pet, raised my concerns. I, like every other expatriate Jamaican, was becoming consumed with concerns about the political developments at home.

At that time, my former husband and I and our three young children were relocated to a small town in West Texas. The company he worked for orchestrated this transfer for him as an industrial engineer. I was now a full-time college student working on my BBA degree and the primary caregiver to our children.

One Sunday I read an article that chronicled the social and political evolution that had taken place in Jamaica during the first two years of Michael Manley's government. The article stated that Manley introduced in-depth policies and programs aimed at economic self-reliance, more social ownership of the island's major industries, and greater independence from the world's large capitalist societies. Though written from an American perspective, the article heightened my awareness that the PNP, under Manley's leadership, was going through a significant ideological redefinition. Now I really got concerned about how this would affect both my family and Jamaica.

There were many other articles in the months ahead. Some in the North American version of Jamaica's *Daily Gleaner* outlined a number of new government programs. These included the PNP's attempt to have greater control over media communications by transforming the Jamaica

Information Service into the Agency for Public Information (API). This new agency was now being used to promote the PNP's new policies and programs.

Then came several more articles about Manley's developing relationship with Cuba's Fidel Castro. There was a newly formed Jamaica-Cuba Joint Commission on Economic, Technical and Cultural Cooperation. A whole set of projects were started by this Commission in areas of agriculture, fishing, education, medicine, science and technology. Jamaican youths were being sent to Cuba to learn new skills, while Cubans came to Jamaica to build, at Cuba's expense, several schools, houses and dams.

Cuban doctors also came to the island to work in hospitals. A small number of Jamaican policemen received training in Cuba on security for VIPs. All this, according to the press, after Manley's policies and procedures had included a retroactive production levy on bauxite in the country. These new policies increased Jamaica's revenues from bauxite sevenfold; but they also cut deeply into the pockets of the large capitalist countries that had been draining the island's resources for their own gain.

Under Michael Manley, Jamaica gained control of its bauxite reserves. And just as I thought, the U.S and other large capitalist societies did not take kindly to this unprecedented move by a small, lesser-developed country. I reflected on an ironic motto used by the island's Tourist Board: "Jamaica, we're more than a beach ... we're a country."

In the midst of this turmoil came another letter from Mass Pet. He wrote that he agreed with Manley's new policies; but he also expressed deep concern about the island's rising crime rate and an ensuing battle from the opposing political party, the JLP. That party was attempting to derail Manley's new social and political programs. Mass Pet's letter also stated Manley just announced that Jamaica was now a Democratic Socialist nation. He expressed concerns over the island's economic situation.

Manley's new programs and social changes had been met with negative international reaction, and the press was having a field day. This resulted in a fall in foreign investments in the island's two major industries — tourism and bauxite. Then came a balance of payments crisis of major proportions in the island, followed by lost jobs, a frustrated population, and more violence in the ghettos of Kingston.

"I'm also very concerned, Olivia, particularly after the last three letters I received from my mother and brother," my husband told me as we discussed the situation.

"What do you mean? You've also been getting letters from your family about deteriorating conditions at home?" I asked.

"Absolutely. My brother wrote in his last letter that they were preparing for tough times and major political violence in Kingston," my husband replied.

"He wrote that there are daily smear campaigns against Manley's democratic socialist regime. The mudslinging has gone to the level where the PNP is now being accused of taking Jamaica into communism, just like Castro did with Cuba."

"But Manley is a socialist, not a communist," I interrupted, with my eyes wide open in disbelief. "Why is the JLP using these vicious scare tactics?"

"Well if you really think about it, Manley has fueled the situation with his persistent quest for closeness with Castro." This reply from my husband was laced with dismay. "I really do not understand why he feels the need to begin getting in bed with Castro, knowing very well that this relationship will not only stir up controversy among strong capitalist upper-class Jamaicans, but also with the U.S. Olivia, America holds the purse strings to the International Monetary Fund, the very agency that Jamaica depends on for financial aid."

With growing anxiety, I responded, "Can you imagine the frustration and near starvation that Jamaica's poor will suffer if Manley pisses off the U.S, and they decide to retaliate by calling the IMF loans or by restricting future funds from going to the island?"

"Don't even go there, Olivia," he said, sharing my concern. "Let's hope that things will calm down soon and that the mudslinging will become an unpleasant memory."

One week later, I received another letter from

Mass Pet. This time I read aloud to my husband. "Miss Olivia, things are getting even more worrisome here. Last week *The Gleaner* reported that fears among Jamaica's elites and middle classes because of recent communism propaganda have been causing a rash of migration off the island to other countries. People are leaving for the U.S. and Canada. I'm concerned about the drain of Jamaica's brainpower off the island. Prominent professionals are leaving us behind because of what I feel are unwarranted fears."

Mass Pet's letter continued, "The Bauxite levy has negatively put Jamaica on the map for U.S. policymakers. And it is reported that Manley's relationship with Cuba has America very concerned. They, of course, view Castro's motives as suspicious. So there are now hostilities from the U.S. against Jamaica, and those of us who are still here fear that Manley's government may be undermined. This would definitely help the JLP, who I fear are not a better choice for the country. By reducing aid to the island and encouraging negative reporting, the U.S. could really hurt our economy, Miss Olivia."

"My God! What will become of Jamaica? How did things get to this level?" I asked, looking up at my husband with dismay.

Then Mass Pet continued his troubling letter, "Miss Olivia, we are gearing up for another election, and I fear that this one will indeed be bloody. There are reports that dangerous weapons are now in the hands of young thugs in Kingston's ghettos, thanks to the JLP. These young men are unemployed, uneducated, and they do not value the lives of others. If things get too crazy, your mother and I are going to stay with friends near Twickenham temporarily until things calm down. At least Portland Cottage is not yet desirable to the gunmen, so we should be safe there."

Then Papa ended this very troubling letter as follows, "But try not to worry Miss Olivia. Your mother and I will do what it takes to ensure our safety. I will try to write again soon."

I had many sleepless nights after reading this letter. The situation in Jamaica had become a focal point for discussions between my husband and me. We read every newspaper and magazine article we could get our hands on. We learned that Michael Manley had won a second term in office after a bloody election during which hundreds were killed. Things were even more worrisome, because there were no letters from Mass Pet for over a month after the election. Attempts to phone home were unsuccessful. I prayed that both he and Miss Birdie were safe.

According to the press, Manley was now counting on significant aid from the Soviet Bloc and from some OPEC countries; but his request for assistance did not have any positive results. So

Manley decided to partner with academics from the island's university to design a program called the People's Production Plan. This plan was aimed at bringing Jamaica closer to economic self-reliance, and included an island-wide, land-lease program available to citizens for developing individual small farms. The plan also included special programs in areas of agriculture, livestock and later on in manufacturing. It stated that these programs were to use raw materials that were available locally and in the region.

As I read this, I was puzzled about how Jamaicans were expected to change their love for foreign goods overnight. Where would the money to put these programs in place come from, especially given the fact that there was also a huge deficit in the country's budget? To top things off, it was also reported that Jamaica's private sector was preparing to pressure Manley to back away from his leftist political activity and rhetoric.

I was relieved as a letter finally came from Mass Pet. I ripped it open and anxiously read its contents aloud. "Miss Olivia, stop worrying. Your mother and I are OK, although I must tell you that we lived through some hairy times. Rumors were flying about the government potentially coming after and taking over 'idle lands' for their national small-farming projects. Now I was really terrified. It was as if I had escaped to Twickenham to have Twickenham escape me. And I wouldn't know how to protect our legacy from a government that may have gone too far."

He continued, "Anyway, there has been no government takeover of private lands. The government has simply pulled together all idle public lands and begun leasing them to small farmers."

Then he continued, "Miss Olivia, you know that I'm an old adventurer who has traveled the world. I have worked in treacherous situations in search of both wealth and a rush of adrenaline. However, I should simply have stayed in Jamaica because the fear and adrenaline rush I am having the displeasure of experiencing here has been unprecedented. And I'm not getting paid a dime for it."

"Your mother and I are back in May Pen," he wrote. "We now live for the next piece of news about Michael Manley's shenanigans and the JLP's counter-reaction."

I held my head up from the letter, sighed deeply, and said to my husband, "I feel so helpless. How do we help our loved ones back home? Do I fly to Jamaica and bring them here to live with us?"

"Olivia, you know that your parents will remain in Jamaica until the lights go out on the island," he shook his head and responded. "My parents feel the same way. We just have to be grateful that the violence has subsided, and that they have survived this mess with their lives intact."

"You're so right," I quickly replied. "But I think

I'll catch a flight to go see them in a few weeks!"

"Please wait a few months until things settle down, Olivia." My husband pleaded. "I need you around to help me raise these children."

During the political upheavals, Bob Marley attempted to bring the two opposing political leaders together at a now famous and courageous reggae concert in Kingston. Gunmen with a political agenda shot Marley, and he reportedly fled to temporary exile in the Bahamas.

And of course, there were more articles in the newspapers and special television announcements. One article attempted to objectively examine the features of Manley's People's Production Plan; but it was clear that the writer viewed the plan with the cynicism that had now become a part of the anxious and exhausted Jamaican psyche. In a later article, this same feature writer outlined the reasons why he predicted that the plan would not come to fruition. Among other things, he claimed, "Jamaicans could not be expected to change their attitudes about luxuries such as foreign goods overnight, especially when they are struggling to survive such hard times."

By coincidence, Mass Pet's next letter stated, "It is now reported that Manley's very ambitious People's Production Plan has fallen by the wayside. He is now gearing up to go to the IMF for another loan. He has already warned the country that this loan, if received, would come with a lot of strings attached. According to Manley, we should now prepare to tighten our belts and get ready for shortages of basic goods, including food items, toiletries and clothing.

"And to top it off Miss Olivia," his letter continued, "there have also been unconfirmed reports that the CIA is now on the island. It is rumored that they have helped the JLP to resist Manley's efforts. America has denied these claims, but I'm beginning to wonder if they have some merit. Many events on the island, and the JLP's leader Seaga's close relationship with Ronald Reagan, make me very suspicious. All it took was for Jamaica to assert its rights to its own bauxite resources in the form of a levy, and we awakened one of the capitalist giants. We may be feeling the effects of America's anger for a long time. Miss Olivia, I could walk through Twickenham pleading to our forefathers for mercy, but I doubt that they can help us now."

Six months later I flew to Jamaica. I had to ship two barrels of food and toiletries ahead of the flight. Shortages of consumer goods on the island included basic necessities like toilet paper, flour, salted cod and rice. Everyone flying there to visit would receive long lists of items from suffering relatives who were now frustrated and in need. A simple trip to the supermarket with Miss Birdie proved to be the experience of a lifetime. I looked around with disbelief at the bare shelves and stood in long lines with a mob of irritated citizens waiting to buy basic goods such as matches or salted mackerel.

Manley lost power to the opposition during the next election. There continued to be strong beliefs on the island that they were victims of both overt and covert foreign intervention.

"We ran the British off with guerilla warfare during the days of slavery," one of Mass Pet's letters wisely summed things up. "But nothing could prepare the small island of Jamaica for the price it would pay for attempting to become economically independent — and for awakening both anger and suspicion in one of the world's largest capitalist giants."

chapter 13

Life is a Battle:
Miss Olivia's Story

ARDSHIPS, SACRIFICES AND A NEAR-
NERVOUS breakdown were soon upon me. I
wondered whether the challenges of living in America
were worth what it took for an island woman to
achieve success in this wonderful land of opportunity.

Several decades ago our Maroon forefathers
fought to free us from the brutality of the
plantations; but nothing could have prepared me for
life as a single parent in America. Marriage to my
first husband had ended, so I tackled the challenges
of raising three young children alone. I took my
share of blame for the breakup. I did not have
the seasoning or maturity to withstand the rigors
of domestic life. Neither did I adjust well to the
constant routines of being a young mother and wife.
Though my husband had his idiosyncrasies, he was

a good man; but now I needed to free myself from the oppression of jealousy and possessiveness that symbolized his love. So when my son and youngest child Christopher was just two years old I decided to go it alone.

Many of my girlfriends played the victim as their own husbands left their sides for life as absentee fathers. They said that I should feel better, because I was actually the one who left my marriage. I was confused by that thought process. Not only was I grieving the loss of a husband, I also had to cope with the guilt that I was the one who walked away. I carried guilt about leaving the man and almost devastating him. I felt guilty about denying my children a full-time father. I agonized about how I would maintain the lifestyle they had become accustomed to regardless of any financial assistance provided by my now-former husband.

Yet I was a resourceful survivor and "warrior" from Twickenham. So I soon bought a four-bedroom home in a middle-class South Miami neighborhood. And the school system was pretty reputable to boot. As I worked to get my new home in order and my children settled into school, I also struggled to find work.

I decided that the only way to maintain my children's lifestyle was to secure a position with a growing company. This way I could climb the corporate ladder while increasing my earning potential. As a recent college graduate with limited corporate experience, the best position available was an entry-level human resource job with a Florida-based bank — this was the field that held my interest for a number of years, so I decided to bite the bullet and apply all clichés like "get my foot in the door," and "tighten my belt," and focus on raising the children.

Don't let my bravado fool you. Life was difficult, stressful, and sometimes borderline impossible. In the islands, a middle-class single mother could afford to pay a maid to do the domestic chores. So one had the luxury of having a responsible adult presence at home when the children arrived from school. There was time for rest and relaxation in the evenings, and occasional weekend family outings to one of the beautiful beaches or resorts on the island.

Besides, one usually had the benefit of an extended family that stepped in and helped raise the children. This supported the philosophy: "It takes a village to raise a child." Family members pitching in included grandparents, aunts, uncles or cousins. Not only did they contribute to the children's growth, they also applied rewards and discipline when necessary. It was all a part of the culture.

Life in America was another story. I had to put my children in an after-school program. And the rush home immediately after work was always frantic. They had to be picked up on time or a late fee would be charged — and this was definitely not in the household budget. Fortunately for both the children and me, they had supervised help with homework at the after-school facility. So now I didn't have to sit up 'till midnight as I helped three children with homework.

Every other Saturday, we went bargain shopping for food so the children would remain well-fed and healthy. Then I spent my entire Sunday cooking three to four dishes and freezing them so they could have healthy homemade hot meals after school. Undoubtedly, the energy level after a long and difficult day of climbing the corporate ladder and fighting the harried Miami traffic was just not there for cooking and cleaning after work. Hence all-day Sunday, I was in the kitchen.

And there were very limited funds for entertainment. So about one weekend per month, I would pack my little troops in the backseat of my compact car and drive 65 miles to Isla Morada in the Florida Keys. At a popular ocean resort there, we would cavort in the pool and the ocean, and then dance and sway together in the sand to the reggae band playing on the beach. On one of these jaunts, I announced at around 7:00 p.m., "I've had enough. Come on kids, let's head home."

My children reluctantly climbed into the car, grumbling and complaining. About 12 miles outside of Isla Morada, my middle child Tanya pleaded,

"Come on Mom, let's go back. We were having so much fun. Pleeease?"

So I turned the car around and cruised back to the reggae band on the beach where we enjoyed more dancing and swaying in the sand until around 1:00 a.m. Afterwards, I carefully drove home, with my clan snoring loudly in the backseat. We were happy. This was an affordable way for us to blow off some well-earned steam, enjoy some bonding, and generally unwind.

My ex-husband and I agreed that the children would spend all summer holidays in Jamaica. Our goal was to get them well connected with their Jamaican roots — we both decided that this was an important part of their development. They could also enjoy being spoiled by their grandparents on both sides of the family. After several years of these summer jaunts in Jamaica, I went to visit Mass Pet and Miss Birdie.

"Miss Olivia, I don't know about these 'Jamerican' (slang for Jamaican-American) children of yours," Mass Pet declared, obviously amused.

"What do you mean Papa?" I responded, now very curious. "How do you think that they are different than we, who grew up on the island?"

Mass Pet smiled and with a very mischievous look, he said, "Here's one example Miss Olivia. Remember when you, Clinton and Dahlia would compete to chop the head off the chicken that we had chosen for Sunday dinner?"

"Of course! How could I forget that?" I laughed with enthusiasm. "We would put the big tin pan that Cookie used to wash our clothes in over the poor chicken's body, with just the head exposed. Then we would count to three, chop the head off with one big swing of the machete, and hide our faces as the body flapped around under the pan. It would flap until it could move no more."

"Ah Miss Olivia," Mass Pet exclaimed. "Then what would happen after that?"

"Then we would bolt through Twickenham, jumping through tall grass and scampering up fruit trees," I quickly responded, my mind racing back in time. "Meanwhile, Cookie would start plucking feathers and dramatically tossing them out through the kitchen window. It was like a ritual."

"Keep going, Miss Olivia," Mass Pet egged me on.

"Soon we were drawn to the most incredible aroma of Cookie's fresh brown-stewed chicken calling us in 'from the wild,'" I reminisced.

"Well Miss Olivia, here's how your Jamerican children handle the farm chickens," Mass Pet said, more mischief in his grin.

"Ha," I giggled, "here it comes."

"They play house with the chickens," Mass Pet teased. "They tie pink ribbons around their necks. They give them names and treat them like human babies."

"OK, then what happens?" Now I was the one egging him on.

"Then Cookie starts flinging fowl feathers through the damn kitchen window," he laughs. "And all of a sudden the children come running into the house bawling and yelling, 'Papa, Papa, Cookie killed Betsie! She killed Betsie and now she's cooking her!'"

By now I'm almost on the floor, writhing with fits of laughter; but Mass Pet was relentless. Trying very hard to control himself, he continued, "Then Miss Olivia, we sit down to a sumptuous dinner of Cookie's succulent fresh brown-stewed chicken with rice and peas and fried plantains. But there were even more bawling and gagging going on as your three Jamerican children bolt through the dining room door in horror, holding their throats with both hands and screaming, 'Poor Betsie! They're eating poor Betsie! Aaaaah!'"

I worked hard to calm myself down from the biggest bellyaching laugh I'd had in years.

"Ah, Papa. Would you believe that many American children have never seen a live chicken?" I commented, holding Mass Pet around the shoulders. "I'm convinced that they think chickens come from the local supermarket!"

"Miss Olivia, the best thing you are doing is to send them home to Jamaica so we can toughen up their little Jamerican backsides!" Mass Pet advised, still laughing his guts out.

On my trip back to Miami, I pondered the irony of Mass Pet's comment about 'toughening up their little Jamerican backsides.' Dealing with the farm chickens was a breeze compared to the lonely rigors of single parenting in the U.S. I had decided to give up any semblance of romance or companionship in my life during these parenting days. I had neither the time nor the energy for it. I also knew that I needed to be careful about the potential dangers my young children could be exposed to. The mere thought of the wrong man at home playing stepdad to them terrified me.

Besides, most of the young men I met had not the maturity, financial stability nor the desire to take on a ready-made family. So life was financially, physically and emotionally challenging. I constantly struggled to satisfy the needs of my Jamerican children, while grappling to make ends meet. The children were wonderful; but growing up in the islands did not prepare me for catering to the emotional needs of American-born children. Many Caribbean parents left home to work abroad. It was the only way for them to support their families. So as a child, you learned to be more emotionally independent, living with grandparents, and looking forward to the beautiful clothes and toys that would arrive in huge packages from Canada, England or America.

My children needed much parenting, and they

looked to me for all of it. Since their father lived in another state, I had little to no help with the everyday demands of raising them.

So I constantly fought against physical, mental and psychological burnout. I also learned a few things about myself in the interim. I needed to be more nurturing; but between my British/Jamaican upbringing, the stresses of single parenting, and the rigors of corporate work, I just didn't have enough to go around. I worried constantly about not being able to pay the bills. I worried about what would become of my children if I were to get sick or die. I worried about holding on to my job. I worried about keeping the children balanced. Worrying had become a daily ritual.

I was also struggling to raise them with West Indian values in an American society. This only increased life's stresses and challenges. I had to learn to balance the need for them to dress for school in the latest designer clothes, while wishing for starched and ironed school uniforms. The British got us accustomed to this in the islands. Then came more anxiety, as I attempted to explain why we could not afford the latest designer fashion, and why they needed to be themselves and not succumb so readily to peer pressure.

Christmases were spent bargain shopping for gifts. We were first in line at 7:00 a.m. at one of the local discount stores. We'd bolt in and scoop up

one of the few remaining designer dolls or video
games, so that the holidays would be enjoyable.
In addition to being mother, father and friend to
the children, I was also Santa Claus at Christmas.
I was determined that they never felt deprived;
but oh how lonely Christmas nights had become,
after everyone was tucked into bed. I would sit
alone in bed staring blankly at the television. I
had unselfishly been Santa Claus to three beautiful
children; but there was no one to be Santa Claus
for me.

After five years of single parenting, the burnout
had really set in. My nerves and stomach began to
rebel. Several trips to the doctor revealed the need
for a temporary escape to recharge my batteries.
So I flew Miss Birdie up from Jamaica to take care
of the children. Then I arrived in Port-of-Spain,
Trinidad, for Carnival with my best friend Diana.
Diana was Trinidadian and a single mother with
two boys. In the States, we cried on each other's
shoulders frequently, as life's pressures sometimes
pounded us into submission.

We arrived in Trinidad two days before Carnival
Monday. Then we spent our days at the calypso
tents where we listened to the new tunes. These
calypsos exploded in the streets during carnival.
Afterwards, they would resonate to the other
islands, and to North America, London and Canada.
After all, the West Indian expatriates also needed

to revel and dance to the latest tunes. At night, we showed up at the calypso competitions all over Port-of-Spain. And we would sing and jam in the north stand at the local stadium at more spirited musical competitions.

On Carnival Sunday morning Diana announced in her deep Trinidadian accent, "Girl, hang on for the ride of your life. We going to 'jouvert' tonight around midnight. And we'll be 'wining' (gyrating) through the streets of Port-of-Spain until about 5:00 a.m. Then we'll head home, sleep for an hour, then off we go to play mas' (masquerade) in the streets all day. You ready my Jamaican friend?"

"Bring it on girl. I came here to unwind," I announced with much anticipation. "Let's go buy two flasks of 'Trini' rum and go absolutely crazy!"

What an experience "jouvert" was! We, dressed in old shorts and skimpy tops, our bodies sweaty and plastered with a mixture of oil and cocoa. As we bumped and grinded through the streets of Port-of-Spain to the pulsating rhythms, I stared at the colors and festivities around us and asked Diana, "Why can't life be like this?'"

There were people of all ages, big grins on their faces, dancing and gyrating to the melodies while sipping on rum. Some were just relishing a natural high as the Afro-Caribbean rhythms percolated through their souls. There were 80-year-old women with their canes doing a jig at every street corner, as the band of revelers danced by with passion and much animation.

It started raining. I announced, "I think I'm going to be sick."

"No girl, just take a big sip of the 'Old Oak' Trini rum and you'll be all right," Diana placated as she handed me a flask.

Boy was she right. The brief tropical shower cooled us off and kept us jamming through the streets 'till the wee hours.

Again we slept for about one hour. Then we bolted out of bed and dressed in full costume Carnival Monday to meet the band at the mas' camp. The biggest and most ornate part of the costume was the headdress. We were playing mas' (masquerade) with one of the largest, most colorful, and elaborate bands in Trinidad's carnival. I quickly learned that when you play mas' in a band, you buy a costume created by the band's designer and dance in the streets all day to the calypsos. Our band had several thousand revelers in skimpy costumes, with huge ostentatious headdresses. The costumes were created around exotic themes, orchestrated by the band's designer and owner.

I looked around at the live soca and calypso bands. They were mounted on top of huge flatbed trucks. The crowd rhythmically pranced through the streets behind these trucks, as infectious harmonies blasted all troubles away. An erotic and rhythmic ritual consumed me. Now completely mesmerized, I allowed my body to go on a natural musical high. I succumbed to the swaying and gyrating for miles and miles through the streets of Port-of-Spain. It was like communing with the ancestors through music and dance.

I reflected on the history of Trinidad's Carnival. The slaves were not allowed to partake in the annual festivities enjoyed by whites during colonial days. So they made musical instruments from the tops of molasses drums, known today as the steel drum. They pounded these drums and danced through the cane fields in their own carnival. These creative creatures also made instruments from the covers of heavy metal pots, which they beat rhythmically with a metal spoon. Trinidadians call this "beating iron." And now during Carnival, the men take great pleasure in gathering in their own groups to "beat iron," as their women enjoy more dancing and gyration in the streets. On my rhythmic journey, I observed many groups of older men "beating iron" from one corner to the next. The smiles on their faces said it all.

By now all stresses were about to leave my body. My senses said, "Just gyrate with the music 'till your body can move no more." I freed myself — life's tensions were melting away. I again looked at Diana, who by now could read my mind. She winked and said, "I know. Why can't life be like this?"

Carnival Tuesday we again danced through the
streets all day, this time without costume. Now
we had more freedom to run from one band to the
other and pause to devour exotic meals at the local
eateries. Then we would chase down the next band
passing by and resume the dancing.

More sights awaited us. After one pause for a
quick snack, we beheld a band of muscular male
revelers gyrating passionately toward us. We
stopped dead in our tracks to take in the many
shades of muscular flesh pulsating in our direction.
They were adorned only with old, cut-off jeans,
sneakers, and big, ornate head dresses. Their chests
were bare and well oiled, and their legs were strong
and relentless. As they pulsated past us, I had to
take my bottom lip off the ground from what I saw
next. The backs of their cut-offs were altered with
large holes that showed their bare behinds. The
letters "VAT" were written on their buttocks. We
jumped in behind them, joined in with the gyrating,
while happily enjoying the view.

"Diana, what the hell does VAT mean?" I asked,
eyes still wide open, lips now off the ground.

"Girl, that's the new 15 percent Value Added Tax,
otherwise known as the VAT tax. The Trinidadian
government has just imposed this on its people," she
replied, bumping, shaking and smiling at the sight
ahead. "The boys are doing an all-out bump and
grind, while baring their asses at the government

in protest. But girl, I ain't complaining, because the view from here could make a woman's imagination run wild!"

Then as our crowd of revelers pranced through one local community, a homeowner took pity and sprayed us down with her garden hose. The idea was to cool us off from the blaring Caribbean sun. She had also cooled us off from the effects of the bare muscular flesh rotating ahead in cut-off jeans.

Everyone was out in the streets that Tuesday. The whole island shut down and the only business was Carnival, Caribbean rhythms, fun, and any animated expression you wanted to conjure up and unload. As Diana and I blended in with the next band coming our way, she pointed out an older man dancing by in what looked like a loincloth. He would have been quite distinguished had it not been for the outfit. She announced that he was the Prime Minister. Then she playfully glanced at the look of disbelief on my face and commented once more, "I know. Again, why can't life be like this? I don't know Miss Olivia. All I can say is enjoy what you can as often as you can. Let's 'wine' our asses off so we can build up the courage to face America in a few days."

Carnival ended abruptly at midnight that night. The next day we drove to Maracas beach with a slew of tired revelers. We picnicked and dozed under a couple of swaying coconut trees, as I struggled to mentally prepare myself for life as a single parent back in the land of opportunity.

Trinidad's carnival left me relaxed and mellow for about three whole months after returning to Miami. I would drive to my stressful corporate job singing the chorus of one of the calypsos that we danced to through the streets of Port-of-Spain.

"Don't bother me now, don't bother me
Don't humbug me now, don't humbug me
Party on fire, carnival fever
I will see you later, you alligator!"

And my children were pleased with the renewed and relaxed "Mommy Olivia." So all my guilt about leaving them behind soon melted away.

One morning later, we were preparing for work and school when my six-year-old son, Christopher, bolted tearfully into my bedroom, moaning that his pet bird Sox was not moving. He grabbed me by the hand and anxiously led me to the scene of his anguish. There he was — poor Sox, flat on his back, feet straight up and dead as nails. We gently laid Sox to rest in an old shoebox. Then I orchestrated a quick bird funeral in the backyard. I proceeded to dig Sox's grave with a shovel, dressed for work in stockings, high heels and business suit. We said goodbye to Sox, holding hands and singing a most mournful hymn. I then had exactly five minutes to explain the concept of death to my three young children before hurrying them off to school. Then I fought the hairy Miami traffic to work.

Three months later the carnival calm had obviously worn off. Diana called me one day in a panic.

"Girl put your foot up my ass because I just killed Grapes," she blabbered in her thickest Trinidadian accent.

"What do you mean you killed Grapes? How could you do a thing like that?" I responded in horror.

"I was in my usual rush to get the boys to school and show up at work on time, so I wouldn't have to deal with my horrible boss," Diana recanted with humorous horror, which is the best way to describe her horror. "Next thing I knew, I backed the damn car right over poor Grapes. The boys began to holler, 'Maaa … you killed Grapes! Aaaaaah!'" she continued.

"Oh my God, poor cat. What the hell did you do at this point?" I responded, in obvious shock.

"We flew out of the car to behold poor Grapes' broken and throbbing body next to the back tire," Diana recounted. "By now the boys were hysterical, and I decided that my boss would have to kill me, but I'm calling in sick because I couldn't leave my boys in this condition."

"Then what the hell did you do?" I again interrupted.

"I started prioritizing real quick like this," Diana answered. "First, take the boys in the house and calm them down. Second, get the best-looking shoebox from the closet and put Grapes' mangled body in it. Third, plan the best cat funeral of the year. Fourth, calm the boys down again and explain accidental death to them before they go nuts!"

"OK, tell me the rest quickly before I'm the one who loses it!" I urged her to keep talking.

"The boys wanted burial by sea, so off we drove to Biscayne Bay sobbing and bawling," Diana's accent was now even deeper. She continued, "I could hardly see the road ahead, girl. The boys by now were hugging the shoebox like they couldn't bear to part with Grapes' mutilated body. I soon pulled the car up on the sand and we got out. Then I wrestled the shoebox out of the boys' frantic grips, and set it 'asail.'"

"Oh my God, now they must really be hysterical!" I commented, eyes protruding.

"No girl, they were calm now," Diana tiredly lamented. "They looked up at me with innocent doe eyes and asked, 'Mommy, can we sing a hymn? Give us a hymn to sing, *please*?'"

I couldn't help it, nor could I understand how something so tragic could have sounded so hilarious. All I could do now was struggle to maintain my calm as Diana continued frantically.

"Well girl, I was still in shock and all my brain could muster up was 'Red Red Wine.' So we pelted out: 'Red

red wine, go to my head, make me forget that I'm
...' as poor Grapes sailed out to sea in the Steve
Madden shoe box."

Then my hysterical Trini friend announced
urgently, "I'm coming over to your house for a shot
of the 190-proof Jamaican rum, before I lose my
mind!"

When the pressure of single parenting got more
intense than she could bear, Diana always sought
solace in the church not the bottle. Friends and
acquaintances constantly led her from one church
to another to relieve her constant search for
inspiration. One day she phoned me and professed,
"Girl, I found the perfect church!"

"Really? How many times have we been down this
road?" I responded with much cynicism. "What is so
great about *this* church?"

"I can't begin to explain it girl." Diana replied
with much excitement. "Just come to service with
me this one time. You'll be filled with so much of the
Holy Spirit, you won't want to leave the building, I
promise."

"Now Diana, you know that I prefer a more
serene and quiet type of worship," I complained,
more skepticism taking over. "My life is crazy
as it is and any attempt to sit through drama in
what's supposed to be the Lord's house, will just
completely finish shattering my nerves."

"Trust me girl — you'll be a different woman

after one service ... ready to take on the entire world," Diana responded exuberantly.

"OK ... but this is the last time I'm going on any church chases with you," I sighed, with both surrender and suspicion. "This time it had better be good."

Diana attempted to open her mouth.

"Oh no," I interrupted. "Don't even bother telling me that you will pick me up. I'm driving my own car so that I can make a quick exit if needed!"

"You damn Jamaicans are so crotchety," Diana taunted. "Just leave it up to a doltish 'Trini' to get you out of your shell."

So off I went the following Sunday morning to Diana's latest shot of the Holy Spirit in South Miami. We met at the church entrance and strolled in together, as Diana quietly greeted "Sister Mary and Brother John." I immediately noticed that these church folks were dressed for some real action.

"Oh great," I thought. "Here we go again with the screaming and blabbering in tongues. Why do I let her sucker me in ... when, oh when will I finally learn?"

The service began with several spirited hymns and some loud hand clapping. Then Mr. Pentecostal preacher went from a calm and threatening sermon, to a loud, booming, thunderous blast of pleadings for atonement to us, the "pitiful sinners."

The woman next to me sprang up from her seat, screaming, "Hallelujah." Then she plopped down on the floor and began fluttering around like an epileptic fit overcame her. And as I glanced ahead at the pulpit, I witnessed several people moving slowly forward, trembling, arms outstretched. Some of them were singing loudly and screaming in yet more tongues.

Then the crowd whipped itself into a frenzy as one middle-aged man screamed, "Asta la doocha, kala ma zita!"

By now two hours had passed, my head was pounding, and I was completely traumatized. I glanced over at Diana. She was now singing and clapping gleefully, like a child touched by a powerful force. I nudged her on the shoulder and exclaimed, "Got to go girl, I got to go!"

I flew out of the church as quickly as you can imagine, jumped into my car, and sped off to a popular local eatery nearby. I grabbed a seat, urgently beckoned the waitress over, and ordered a double vodka and tonic. The young waitress looked at me curiously and asked, "Are you OK? You look like you've been run over by a freight train. Where are you coming from?"

"Church, I'm coming from church, for God's sake!" I growled with agitation and exhaustion.

The waitress walked away shaking her head with bewilderment. I sighed and thought, between long sips of the double vodka, "Inspiration my foot! That kind of noise and commotion could cause a woman some serious stress and trauma. I think I'll stick with my own form of serene communing with the Lord, thank you very much!"

chapter 14

A Trip to Cuba

THE MYSTERIES OF CUBA RETURNED
with tests of courage, despondent eyes and daring
escapes. And this time, I experienced it firsthand,
in Cuba.

During the summer of 1989 I flew to Jamaica with
my three children, Charlene, Tanya and Christopher.
They chatted with anticipation and excitement about
another holiday with their loving grandparents and
about more rich cultural explorations. Twickenham's
emblem showed itself to us after a long drive
from the airport. The children bolted from the car,
embraced Miss Birdie and Mass Pet, and quickly
changed clothes. Then they took off like animals just
freed from capture. They raced through tall grass,
climbed up mango trees, and filled their bellies with
succulent ripe fruit just like I did as a child.

I, too, finally began to relax. Then Miss Birdie joined me over a tall glass of brown-sugar lemonade on the veranda where she announced, "I'm glad you're here, Miss Olivia. I want to talk with you about something very exciting." She had a look of sheer delight on her face.

"What's going on, Mama?" I asked, now very curious.

"I received communication from our family in Cuba," she replied with a rush of emotion.

"How absolutely exciting!" I interrupted. "Who contacted you? Is Aunt Suzie alive? What's going on with the family there?" I couldn't stop the questions from flowing.

"Whoa, Miss Olivia! Slow down." Miss Birdie immediately responded. "Here's what happened. The son of one of your father's old friends took a job in Guantanamo Bay. He works as a civilian at the U.S. Naval Base there."

I again interrupted. "Really! I had no idea that Jamaicans were now traveling to Cuba to work at the base. How long has this been going on? How do they get to the island — by boat or by plane?"

"Jamaicans have been working there for a number of years," Miss Birdie continued. "They commute by plane to and from Cuba as civilian workers. I hear that they get paid very well — and in American dollars too. And you know how strong the U.S. dollar is compared to our currency."

"Go on! Let's get back to Papa's friend." I responded anxiously.

"Yes ... anyway your father's friend's son Mike came back to Jamaica after a six-month working stint in GITMO ... that's what he calls Guantanamo Bay," Miss Birdie continued, hoping for fewer interruptions this time. "He told his father about a conversation he had with his Cuban boss, a man named Patrick Sanchez ..."

"Wait a minute, wasn't Aunt Suzie's married name Sanchez?" I again jumped into the conversation. Now I was overcome with excitement. "Oh my God, Mama is that one of her sons?"

"Calm down girl and let me finish the story, will you?" Miss Birdie again protested. "This Patrick Sanchez told him that his mother constantly grieved about the family she left in Kingston, Jamaica, and how she got stuck in Fidel's revolution and was never able to see them again."

"Go on!" I urged.

"Mike had several more conversations with Sanchez about his Jamaican family," Miss Birdie continued. "Then prior to his most recent trip back to Jamaica, Patrick Sanchez begged Mike to try and locate the family he never met."

By now, all juices were flowing at full speed. I again interrupted, "Hurry up and get to the punch line ... I'm dying here, Mama!"

"Have patience child ... I'm getting there." Miss

Birdie calmly continued. Oh, how she loved to drag out a story. "Anyway, as your father listened to this his 'antenna' was working full-time. He suddenly realized that Patrick Sanchez was Aunt Suzie's son who had disappeared after the revolution, attempting to escape to Florida. Remember that the family thought sharks ate Patrick at sea. He was never seen nor was he heard from after that."

"Oh my God, this is incredible!" I shrieked.

"And to top it off, there was an order to shoot and kill him if he showed up again in Cuba after the escape attempt," Miss Birdie continued relentlessly. "But the plot thickens, Miss Olivia. Mike handed your father a sealed envelope that Patrick Sanchez had given him to pass on to a potential family member in Jamaica."

"*Jesus* Mama, let me see the letter before I explode. I must see the letter!" I demanded.

Miss Birdie jumped up and retrieved the letter from a bureau drawer in her bedroom. She handed it over to me. I sighed with relief as I eagerly opened it and saw that it was written in English. I began to read the letter out loud.

"*My Dear Jamaican Family:*

My name is Patrick Sanchez, and my mother's maiden name is Suzie Thomas. My mother migrated to Cuba from Jamaica in the 1950s to join my father, whose name is Reuben Sanchez. My mother talked constantly about her mother and father, her sisters

Viola and Dolly, and her brothers Patrick and Eric.

If you are or are related to one of these individuals, I am anxious to meet you. I need to stop wondering about my Jamaican family. I want the opportunity to meet and get to know them in person.

Please send a letter to me with Mike, and I will respond promptly. With loving memories attained from the lips of my mother and with much anticipation.

Patrick Sanchez."

I grabbed Miss Birdie's arm and yelled, "My God Mama! It's Uncle Patrick. He's alive. Did you respond yet? When are you going to visit?"

"I sent him a long letter about the family, which should make him comfortable about who I really am," Miss Birdie replied, calm as usual. "I'm waiting for Mike to return with a reply."

"OK ... but when are you going to Cuba?" I persisted.

"I'm going to plan a visit as soon as I get a response. I'm hoping also to be able to meet the rest of the family there, God willing." Miss Birdie said, with much anticipation.

Three months after my return to the United States, Miss Birdie wrote that Mike had delivered a letter to her from Uncle Patrick in Guantanamo Bay. In the letter, he talked about the family in Cuba. He expressed deep sadness that he had never been allowed to see his dear mother since his escape over 20 years ago. There was a devastating emptiness in his life because of this. So meeting his Jamaican family would fill a huge void, he wrote.

Uncle Patrick included in the letter a special pass on one of the many military flights between Cuba and Kingston, Jamaica. These flights take U.S. Navy men and Jamaican civilian workers back and forth between both islands. Miss Birdie was scheduled to fly to GITMO to meet Uncle Patrick and his family within the next two weeks.

I was very anxious to hear about my mother's trip to Cuba. These series of events were really thrilling to me. I thought about how ironic life was and about how things can come full circle. Here we were, thinking that poor Uncle Patrick died at sea. Then over 20 years later he shows up out of the blue as Mike's boss. What a small world it is indeed.

One month later, I was reading a letter from Miss Birdie, in which she described her trip to Guantanamo Bay. She wrote about the incredible hospitality shown to her by Uncle Patrick and his family. She was impressed with the facilities made available to everyone who lived and worked at the U.S. Naval Base there. She urged me to go and visit my Cuban family as soon as possible. They were anxious to know the rest of our family. I was to call Uncle Patrick, who had already made arrangements for a special visitor's pass for me to fly from

Kingston to Guantanamo Bay. He was waiting to hear from me to confirm the date of my arrival.

On August 27, 1989, I set out on my trip to Guantanamo Bay to meet Uncle Patrick and the family. The journey had me flying from Miami to Kingston, and then waiting to board a flight from Kingston to Guantanamo Bay. As I stood in line at the check-in, I noticed that there were no other women around. So off I went on board the flight with 74 men vying for my attention. They asked to carry by bags, offered me a seat, and told me how good it was that I was aboard. They were Navy men in civilian clothes returning from a long, fun weekend on Jamaica's North Coast. There were also Jamaican men traveling back to work after spending time with their families. And there were Navy men in full uniform reporting to duty. I thought, "Great, this will be an amazing trip — me flying with half the men in GITMO." My only regret was that the trip was only 25-minutes long.

We landed at the airport off of Guantanamo Bay and my cousin Ebony greeted me with open arms. Then we boarded a ferry to the mainland. During that short ride, two things stuck in my mind: how beautiful Ebony was; and how incredible the scenery was. The sky was a light blue, there were puffs of plump, white clouds drifting atop of us, and dozens of dolphins did a merry dance next to the ferry as we sailed along. I was both fascinated and excited.

Ebony had beautiful long brown hair, olive skin, and a gorgeous face. She was gracious and playful. We bonded right away, as she teased me relentlessly about arriving in great style, "like a Jamaican diva," with over 70 men vying to escort me off the aircraft.

We drove in a large, older-model American car at the 25 mph speed limit to a large trailer that housed the family. I learned that most of the inhabitants of GITMO lived in nice trailer homes. And soon there he was — a smiling Uncle Patrick with arms outstretched waiting to greet me. After a huge hug, my long-lost uncle took me inside to meet his wife Mercy. She spoke only Spanish, but she smiled warmly and welcomed me with a loud, "Mi casa es su casa!" Then she escorted me to a very comfortable bedroom, which would be my resting place for the week.

Uncle Patrick was a very youthful 61 year old. He held a critical post as the Chief of Security at the base. It was because of this position that the special visitors' passes were made possible. He was also D.J. at the Officers' Club on base on Friday and Saturday nights, where he played R&B and other classic dance music to entertain the officers and their dates.

GITMO is a small U.S. Navy town on one edge of Cuba. All activities revolve around the base, including entertainment and commerce. I had

arrived on a Saturday, so after a special dinner
of goat meat simmered in beer (Aunt Mercy was
told that Jamaicans like goat meat), Ebony and
I got dressed up and drove to the Officers' Club
with Uncle Patrick. We flirted with the officers
and danced the night away as he played the latest
tunes to keep the party going. That Sunday we
picnicked at the beach. It was arid and rocky — I
hadn't experienced a beach like this in any of the
other Caribbean islands. And to top it off, I spent
half the day up on top of a beach table, terrified of
our beach companions — huge iguanas that came
scampering up to us begging for watermelon. My
cousin laughed and teased when she learned that
Jamaican women are petrified of lizards.

Ebony and I enjoyed hanging out and sharing
some of our life's stories. We also shopped at the
commissary for bargains. Ten years younger than
me, she was fun loving and delightful. Her older
sister Sandy had married a Peruvian and moved
away. I seemed to have temporarily filled the shoes
of older sister for the week.

Later on I spent one important and full day with
Uncle Patrick. During this quality time, he shared
the most fascinating and painful stories with me
about his life in Cuba.

"Olivia," he said, "after the revolution, I had
quickly grown frustrated with the new oppressive
political system. So one evening, in desperation, I

took to the sea on a large inner tube. I knew that if I got caught I would have been shot dead."

"My God, Uncle Patrick, you must have been terrified!" I exclaimed.

"By then, I just didn't care." He commented, staring blankly ahead. "I would have preferred a bullet in my chest rather than having to live under the new regime."

"And you left your wife and young daughter and traveled alone on a mere inner tube, in the middle of the ocean? That really is desperation!" I commented.

"I was doing it for them, Olivia. I wanted my family to have more freedom than I did when I was growing up," he replied. "The thought of my daughter being raised under the conditions we had to endure gave me courage and motivation. I was prepared to risk my life for this thing called freedom."

"Fascinating ... please continue, Uncle Patrick," I urged him.

"I spent three horrible days at sea. I was burned to a crisp by the sun at daytime, and the sharks were circling me at night."

"*Jesus*," I commented, scared to death.

"At dawn on day three, I spotted land. I mustered up the last ounce of strength in my body and paddled furiously with my hands toward what I thought was Florida."

"Olivia, before then I thought death was near," Uncle Patrick recounted. "The few pieces of dry provisions I had with me had either run out or fallen into the sea for the fish to devour. I prayed out loud that it wouldn't attract the sharks. My skin was bloody from the scorching sun and salt water. And I was getting disoriented from being out in the elements so long with no protection," he continued, his faced now riddled with pain.

"Oh, Uncle Patrick, this is the bravest thing I've ever heard," I responded. He had my full attention now.

"I must have passed out from exhaustion when the tube that carried my aching body for three whole days hit the shoreline."

"What happened then?" I asked, my face now reflecting his pain.

"Next thing I felt was the barrel of a gun pressing on the scorched skin of my aching forehead. Two uniformed white men were staring down at me with blank, red faces."

"*Jesus!* What did they do to you?" I asked, wide-eyed and terrified.

"After some interrogation, they dragged me to a Jeep nearby and hoisted me in the backseat," he responded calmly. "I screamed in sheer agony as my sunburned back hit the car seat."

"They then drove me to a nearby military hospital for treatment," he continued.

"You were very lucky to have ended up here," I said, wondering where he found the strength to endure the whole ordeal. "I'm not sure that you would have survived the long trip to Florida alone on an inner tube."

"I guess I was lucky," he responded wearily. "I do admit though to thinking, when I realized I was in Guantanamo Bay, 'My God, I still didn't make it out of damn Cuba.'"

"Uncle Patrick, how did your wife get here?" I asked. "How long after your arrival was she able to escape? I assume she escaped with your older daughter Sandy in tow?"

"It took me two years to mastermind their escape," he responded, voice now wearier that ever. "By then Sandy was only five years old, and it was almost impossible to find someone willing to take the treacherous trip with them. And I knew that they would never have made it alone."

He sighed deeply and then continued, "I managed to get a message across the border to an old friend of mine named Jose Hidalgo. Jose also wanted to escape, so he decided to take the risk and attempt to leave with both Mercy and Sandy."

"You must have been really petrified at this point," I commented, my eyes bulging.

"Olivia," he replied, "I was a blubbering idiot when I realized they would be on their way. All I could think about is how I would ever be able to forgive myself if my wife and baby girl were killed. But by the grace of God they arrived. They were sunburned and disoriented, but they were alive. And poor Jose was right there by their sides."

"You must have said a few prayers that night!" I exclaimed.

"I thanked God all night long. Then I took Hidalgo in and cared for him for several years. He was finally able to get his green card, get work, and find a place of his own."

"What a terrible ordeal. What became of your three brothers and your mother, Aunt Suzie?" I asked, mesmerized by the story.

A deep and terrible sadness took my uncle over. Then he responded, with tears gushing from his eyes. "My mother died last August, and I was not allowed to see her, attend her funeral, or to say goodbye."

"Oh Uncle Patrick, what a painful burden to bear," I responded.

"It has been over 20 years since my escape, Olivia, and my only true regret is that I never got to see my mother ever again."

I reached out and gently squeezed his hand. He continued, more sorrow in his eyes. "I received word in 1984 that my youngest brother Luis was shot dead trying to escape. I never got to say goodbye to him either. It's so hard to be happy when those agonizing events take over your life. All I have now are my wife and two girls. My brothers Juan and Reuben I get to see occasionally."

"How are you able to see them? Don't they still live on the communist side of the island?" I asked quickly.

"They both work at the base here," he looked at me sadly and responded.

"How are they able to work here at the base when they still live on the communist side?" I asked, again very surprised.

"Oh they serve a purpose all right," my uncle responded. "They each are ordered to take six retirement checks across the border every month-end. That is why they are allowed to continue working here at the base."

"Whose retirement checks are they taking across the border?" I asked, now really curious.

"Many Cubans from the communist side of the island have worked here at the U.S. Naval Base for years," he responded. "When they retire, they receive about $1,000 U.S. dollars per month in retirement money. Juan and Reuben collect the checks at month-end, take them across the border, and deposit them into one of the government banks."

"OK, so the retirees get their money from these banks?" I asked.

"They get only a small portion of their money," he snickered. "The bank gives them 1,000 pesos. The rest of their hard-earned retirement money goes to Castro's government," he answered.

"Are you joking? That is unbelievable," I commented.

"But it gets worse, Olivia. Every day when my brothers go across the border they are strip-searched ... both morning and evening."

"Are Uncles Juan and Reuben allowed to visit you?" I asked, now truly disturbed. "When can I meet them?"

"They cannot visit me," he responded, again with a deep sadness in his eyes. "Although they work just a few miles from here, I'm only allowed supervised visits with them at their places of work on the base."

"Could you arrange one of those visits before I leave, so I can see them?" I asked.

"Yes, I'll try for the day after tomorrow," he sighed.

My visit with Uncles Juan and Reuben at their place of employment left me feeling even more uneasy. I was allowed a half-hour with both of them. Uncle Patrick interpreted, because they spoke only Spanish. They both seemed distant and ill at ease. The sadness and emptiness in their eyes were very disheartening. Even their communication with their brother Patrick was distant and emotionless.

Our visit was chaperoned, and I had so many questions, but the environment was not conducive to asking them. I was most struck by how much they looked alike. They also looked like Uncle Kenrick, Aunt Doll's son. They were tall, handsome and brown-skinned with curly hair. Uncle Juan had our great grandmother's baby blue eyes. Oh, how I wish I could bring smiles to their beautiful-and-empty faces.

On the flight to Miami from Kingston, I reflected on GITMO and my Cuban family. I was left with two feelings: one of warmth, with some degree of closure; and the other feeling was of sadness and compassion for uncles Juan and Reuben, who seemed so distant, and reserved. I was suddenly grateful for the freedom I had taken for granted; freedom to make my own choices in life; and freedom to be a positive influence in the lives of my children. I felt a new sense of gratitude for the life I was returning to in the United States.

chapter 15

The Black Butterfly

*D*EATH KEPT CALLING US, AND WE WERE eventually overcome. Parson Mitchell once preached that death is the only thing that we are guaranteed; but we are never ready for it. Neither can we embrace it, though it may bring an end to pain and suffering. And oftentimes it saturates our souls with anguish, distress and even fear.

I was home alone in South Florida late one Sunday morning. After a light breakfast, an unrelenting ring of the telephone abruptly interrupted my spiritual meditation. On the other end was the voice of my older brother, Maxie, calling from White Plains, New York. Maxie had lived there with his wife Vera for a number of years. After a brief brotherly greeting, his voice took on an urgency unlike any I'd ever heard. My brother sadly uttered, "Miss Olivia, I'm calling to ask for some money to help pay for the doctor bills I'm about to incur."

"Of course," I responded. "What's wrong? Are you sick? You never call me for money!"

"I've been having these awful pains in my lower back," he answered. "The doctors can't seem to figure out what's causing them."

"Have you tried the usual remedies for back pain like hot and cold packs, a good massage, soaking in a hot bath with Epsom salt?" I asked with concern. "I get those every now and then, because of a fall I took when I was a gymnast in Jamaica ..."

"Nothing works, Miss Olivia," he interrupted in distress. "The pain is deep inside of me. It's like nothing I've ever felt. If I ever needed your help, my sister, it is now."

I immediately wired the funds to him; but a couple of days later his wife Vera called and advised that Maxie had been hospitalized. After several phone conversations with him in the hospital, Vera called two days later to say that Maxie was feeling better and would be released the next day. I immediately phoned and told him how happy I was that he was feeling better. I encouraged him to take better care of himself once he got back on his feet. I did not know it then, but this was the last time I would ever hear my brother's voice.

Early the next day, I received a call from my

brother Clinton. He gently asked me to sit down. He announced that Maxie died early that morning. I was at work, and the news hit me like a ton of bricks. All I could do was slump over my desk and weep like an injured child.

In a phone conversation with Maxie's wife afterwards, she revealed the following while sobbing uncontrollably. "I received a call at around 4:00 a.m. this morning from Maxie, asking me to come to the hospital right away. I jumped into a taxi and hurried to his side. When I arrived, he told me that he had lost control of his bowels and wanted no one else to touch him."

Vera was a trained nurse, and I expressed my gratitude, "I'm so glad you were there for him."

"I immediately proceeded to clean him up in bed," she continued, between sobs. "I was glad to do this for my husband," she continued. "I smiled as I turned him on his side, because I knew how self-conscious he could be."

"As I turned him back over from his right side," she recanted, now sobbing even more loudly, "his eyes rolled over into his head. He died right there in my arms, Olivia!"

Now Vera was crying hysterically. She lamented, "We've been together for over 40 years, and I'm lost without him. How am I supposed to go on living without him in my life? Tell me, how?"

Despite my own grief, I made several attempts

to console her. Nothing worked — and now I was overcome by my own sorrow. My boss walked by, heard me weeping, tried to console me, and then sent me home to help with family arrangements.

We flew Maxie's body to Jamaica for burial at Miss Birdie's beloved Port Royal, a peninsula just outside of Kingston. Without a doubt, we knew that this would have been Miss Birdie's wish. Vera had already held a memorial service in White Plains for him, so that his close friends there could say their goodbyes.

When we got to Jamaica, and as we prepared Miss Birdie and Mass Pet for the long trip to Port Royal from Twickenham, Dahlia pulled me aside and shared an observation. She was a retired registered nurse in New York, so we trusted her opinions on health issues. "Olivia, I'm concerned," Dahlia said. "Mass Pet does not look well."

"What do you mean?" I asked, staring deeply into her eyes with concern. "He does seem a little off-balance, but I thought he may be having some vertigo issues. He's had these in the past. Please do not tell me that you suspect something else is wrong."

"I don't like what I'm seeing," Dahlia held me by the shoulders and answered. "Both of his ankles are swollen. This is not a good sign."

"Oh Dear Lord," I responded, now very fearful. Clinton joined us and looked on, his eyes protruding with worry.

"I don't think that Papa can take the long trip to Port Royal for the funeral," Dahlia continued.

"But Sis, he'll strongly resist if we try to prevent him from attending Maxie's funeral," I interjected.

"Olivia, I don't think Papa is strong enough to resist us," Dahlia responded. "Let's go say our goodbyes to Maxie. Then let's head back home immediately and tend to our father."

So we left our loving Mass Pet in the care of the maid. Then we gave Maxie a mournful send off in the church at Port Royal where the infamous old pirate Captain Morgan is buried. Miss Birdie had asked that we bury Maxie in Port Royal's cemetery by the ocean. This is where she had put her mother, aunt and uncles to rest years ago. And here she was, putting yet another of her children in the ground. She did her usual burial ritual. My mother stood over the grave singing loudly, with her illustrious operatic voice — that voice was now much stronger than she had become physically. My heart ached for Miss Birdie. I watched sadly, as her frail body rocked to and fro, and she belted out one hymn after the other. She was courageous, as she sent her oldest child off to his maker.

We embarked immediately afterwards on the long road trip back to Twickenham. I reflected deeply and sadly on our goodbyes to our older brother; but my mind consistently fast-forwarded to Mass Pet's condition at home. I've always known my father to be strong, thin and muscular. He was blessed with a positive, sweet and adventurous spirit. He had consistently been there for me through the good times and through adversity, never judging, always supporting, and helping me face life's challenge. I quietly prayed that he would survive whatever it was we were about to face. I begged God to keep him around for a very long time to come.

We drove through Twickenham's gates at around 9:00 p.m. that night. The family sat down to a late dinner of brown-stewed chicken, rice, fried plantains and brown-sugar lemonade. Mass Pet had eaten earlier and was resting. We spoke quietly about Maxie's life, reflecting positively on the good times. We tried hard not to let the grief and pain overcome us.

"My husband was so talented," Vera said admiringly. "He would lovingly repair the cars of all his friends. They would take it to the dealers, and then to him because they couldn't afford to pay dealer rates."

"Are you kidding? Maxie could raise any piece of old junk from the dead!" Clinton exclaimed between bites. "He would spend a whole day in the belly of any car. It didn't matter whether it was a Ford or a Toyota. Then he would finally emerge covered with grease, motioning you over and instructing you to get in and start the engine. Without a doubt, after two turns of the key, you'd hear the engine of that baby begin to purr. Then he'd have a huge gleam in his eyes, as he wiped the grease from his hands and listened keenly to the engine."

"Yeah, he'd listen to that engine like it was music to his ears," I interjected. "And if you were family you had to be forceful, as he passionately refused to accept payment for his work. He'd come at you with the usual, 'No man, getting this baby to purr is payment enough!'"

"Tell me something I don't know," Vera added with a painful smile. "He also said this to many of his friends, and some took real advantage of his kindness. Then I'd have to get on their backs to collect the money owed so that we could balance the shop's books and pay our other bills. He was a kind soul without a single drop of business sense."

"He was the kindest child I had ... always helping me," Miss Birdie commented after listening keenly. "He would give the shirt off his back to anyone in need. Oh how I will miss him!"

"You know, the doctors think that he died of an aneurism, but they'll know for sure when the results of the autopsy are released," Vera sighed, fighting back more tears.

Dahlia reached over and gave her hand a compassionate squeeze as we continued eating and reflecting.

Then like an abrupt tug on our grieving hearts, we beheld Mass Pet staggering toward us from his bedroom. His eyes were weary, and he was completely disoriented. Clinton sprang from his chair, grabbed him, and yelled, "Papa, are you OK? What's wrong ... are you in pain?"

Our father groaned and began to rip the t-shirt from his thin frame with his bare hands. Dahlia bolted from her chair toward him, held her palm to his forehead, and pulled his eyelids up as she peered closely into both of his eyes. He continued to flail about as Clinton struggled to hold him steady.

"Let's go. We're taking him to May Pen hospital right now," Dahlia instructed with urgency. "Olivia, grab a few of his pajamas, underwear and slippers from the bureau drawer. Throw them into the black bag over there."

Clinton lifted Mass Pet's frail frame up and quickly carried him toward the car. Vera opened the backdoor, and we hoisted him in. We drove frantically for 15 miles to the hospital. Mass Pet groaned agonizingly, as the car sped over unending bumps and potholes in the rough country roads between Portland Cottage and the nearby town of May Pen.

Our father was immediately admitted into the hospital. As they took him away, I couldn't stop weeping. I was grieving our recent loss, and now I was fearing for Mass Pet's fate. I looked on in pain at the strong and adventurous soul I knew and loved, slumped over into a wheelchair — he looked delicate and vulnerable as the nurse wheeled him away.

We had a family meeting after breakfast the next day. We decided that Dahlia and I would stay in Jamaica for the next week to ensure Mass Pet got the best medical care available. The others would return to the U.S. within the next two days as originally planned. Dahlia had previously taken an early retirement from the county hospital in Brooklyn where she worked as a nurse for 28 years. So she didn't need an employer's permission for her extended stay. I called my boss, explained the situation, and was able to remain in Jamaica to help care for our beloved Mass Pet. Clinton would return the rental car in Kingston after driving the other family members to board their respective flights. I was no longer comfortable with doing the treacherous left-hand drives on Jamaica's narrow and winding roads. So Dahlia and I planned to commute back and forth from the hospital by bus or taxi.

The next week was completely dedicated to Mass Pet. Dahlia and I rose early, ate breakfast, and rode to the hospital to help take care of him. We would stop off at May Pen's farmers market to buy fresh bananas, papayas, watermelon slices and energy drinks. Dahlia would continue on the commute to the hospital armed with fresh foods, while I ran around the town center doing Mass Pet's banking and paying Twickenham's utility bills.

I would later join Dahlia at the hospital, where she busily gave Mass Pet his daily bed bath and issued instructions to the local nurses for his medication and lab tests. And our poor father did not make it easy. He frequently attempted to yank the IV needle from his arm and yelled, "I want to go back home to Twickenham so I can die in peace. Take me home to Twickenham, away from this god-forsaken place and these bloody people, please Miss Olivia."

My heart was ripped out of my chest by the look in Mass Pet's eyes as he pleaded with us. So each day we would promise to take him home after the next set of tests were run; but our goal was to get him the best treatment available. At night, my sister and I cried ourselves to sleep out of sheer exhaustion, grief and fear.

One week later, we honored Mass Pet's wishes and took him home. We hired a live-in caregiver to provide for his basic needs and arranged for both a visiting nurse and doctor to give in-home medical care.

Dahlia and I returned to the United States, feeling sad and petrified. I had difficulties balancing grief over the loss of my older brother with dread over the potential loss of my beloved father. Much time was spent on the phone to Jamaica to check on Mass Pet's condition and care. Dahlia, Clinton and I now shared the expenses for his care. We decided to retain the funds he had in his local bank accounts and use the interest to cover everyday expenses.

One month later, Mass Pet was again hospitalized. We flew to his side once more. After this, he repeatedly pleaded with us to let him stay in his own home at Twickenham; so we ramped up the nursing care and in-home medical visits.

Just one month later, a call came from Jamaica that Mass Pet's condition had worsened. In an urgent conference call, my siblings and I decided that Clinton would fly to Jamaica alone to assess the situation and apprise us by phone. A day later, Clinton called and advised, sadly and despondently, that I needed to fly home immediately.

"Miss Olivia," my brother said, "I wish I could tell you that Mass Pet may make it, but I cannot. He is calling for you. You must come home to Twickenham right now."

I boarded a flight to the island that afternoon. It was 5:00 p.m. when I arrived at Twickenham and rushed to my father's side. There he was, my beloved Mass Pet, disoriented, thin as a rail, laying in bed in a cotton shirt and an adult diaper. He stared blankly at me. I held him in my arms and rocked him back and forth, as he muttered almost incomprehensively.

"I'm sailing on a beautiful blue sea in a gorgeous sailboat with crisp, white sails ..."

"We're sailing on that beautiful boat together, Papa," I responded, rocking him to and fro. It was clear to me that he was traveling away from us.

"It's Miss Olivia, and I'm here with you. Everything will be fine now," I comforted him.

Mass Pet left this Earth, in my arms, at around 2:00 a.m. the next morning. I kissed his lifeless mouth. His face relaxed, and he was now at peace. I pulled the white sheet up and covered his motionless body. Then Miss Birdie and I read the Psalms and prayed aloud until dawn. We were at Twickenham in rural Portland Cottage, Clarendon. There were no phone lines, and my cell phone had no reception. I had taken a taxi there from the airport, so I had to wait until dawn before I could get to a phone.

I glanced at the clock, and it was 5:00 a.m. I headed out on foot to our cousin Ralph's home about a mile away. Ralph had a special cell phone that works in rural areas. I called the undertaker; I called Dahlia; and I called Clinton. I delivered the news and instructed them to share it with the rest of the family. I rushed back to Twickenham, Miss Birdie, and the body of my beloved Papa. I was then brought right back to my roots and culture at its most basic level. There were about to be some sobering reminders that, regardless of how many years I lived abroad, I was Jamaican through and through.

I opened Twickenham's gates and hurried through them. For the life of me, I could remember nothing about the walk back. The maid had prepared breakfast, but nothing would pass through my throat. My stomach was in a huge knot and though

I wanted to explode, I could muster up no tears. I looked at Mass Pet laying peacefully in his bed. I caressed his beautiful face, ran my fingers through his straight and silky white hair, and still there were no tears. He was as cold as ice. Then our maid Betty walked in and yanked me away from my beloved father's bedside. Like a child, she led me by the hand to the back veranda and sat me down.

"Miss Olivia," she said sympathetically, "you sure you don't want some of the hot corn-meal porridge I just made? I sweetened it with condensed milk and spiced it up with fresh vanilla and grated nutmeg … just like you always liked it."

"No Betty, I couldn't eat a thing right now … but thanks," I muttered, staring straight past her. "Make sure that Miss Birdie eats a bowl when she wakes up. She must have just fallen asleep; we were up all night, you know."

"OK Miss Olivia." Betty said, patting me on the shoulder reassuringly. "The undertakers will soon get here, don't you worry. Just sit there, and I'll bring you a cup of tea."

Then Twickenham's big iron gates squealed open and a vehicle drove slowly through. It was the undertakers. As they put Mass Pet's body on a stretcher, I busily directed them to be gentle, because that was my Papa they were taking away.

I watched as they put my father's body, now completely covered with a white sheet, into the back of the hearse. I could no longer see his face. My numbness crumbled, and I lost control. I grabbed onto my father's lifeless feet with both hands. Then I screamed with the most painful agony ever experienced. I must have awakened her. The next thing I remembered was Miss Birdie's comforting words, "All right Miss Olivia! Don't cry so hard. Your Papa is at peace now. He is in the Lord's hands. Come with me my child."

Betty and Miss Birdie both sat my trembling body down on the veranda and worked painstakingly to console me. They held me down, and I watched in agony as the hearse drove slowly through the gates of Twickenham with the body of my beloved Mass Pet. Both arms outstretched, I screamed for them to bring him back to me.

Then three men immediately appeared at the entrance of the veranda. They trudged past me directly into Mass Pet's bedroom. Through tearful eyes, I recognized them. They were my father's best friends Joe, Will and Gladstone. Joe was jet black with the sharp-and-intense features of a Maroon. Will was Jamaican of East Indian decent, with straight white hair and a quick gait. Gladstone, dressed in the rustic clothes of a poor countryman, had the demeanor of a free-and-proud African. I don't know where the following thoughts came from, but my pained and weary heart said, "You're home, Olivia. And now you'll be guided by three creatures of Twickenham's roots — a Maroon, a slave and an Indian indentured servant."

Dazed, I followed them into the house and watched mindlessly. They stripped the sheets and pillowcases from Mass Pet's deathbed, and they turned the mattress over in a gentle yet coordinated ritual. Then they carefully led me back onto the veranda and uttered the following instructions.

"Miss Olivia, your father needs you to be strong now. Go to the family's burial ground, which is close to the foundation of your grandmother Sedith's house. Take the greatest care and pick the exact location where your father's grave must be dug."

I looked up at them wearily, gasping for breath between sobs. They continued. "You cannot make any mistakes. If you do, you run the terrible risk that the bones of one of your fore parents may be dug up in error. That would be an awful curse on your Papa, Miss Olivia."

I tried to pull myself together and continued to listen intently.

"Then you must hire the grave diggers," they instructed. "We will help you with that. It will take three days for them to dig the grave and build the tomb."

"What do I do after that?" I asked, looking deep into the eyes of Will, the Indian.

"Once the concrete dries," he replied, "Derek

Davis' son, John, will paint and decorate the tomb for you."

"He can also inscribe any Psalm or Bible verse you want on the walls of the tomb," said Gladstone, the "free and proud African." "Derek does a beautiful job with this, Miss Olivia. You won't be disappointed."

As I listened to this, I struggled to pull myself out of the sea of devastation that I was drowning in. It was critical that I get to work and begin planning my beloved father's sendoff while Clinton, Dahlia, and the rest of the family flew in from America. Then they too would take part in this fascinating and painful ritual.

So off I went to our family's burial ground with Joe, Will and Gladstone in tow. I was as ready as I would ever be, to pick Mass Pet's final resting place. I stared intensely at the gravesites, taxing my brain, and jogging all childhood memories. Sedith would walk me through the site, showing me the unmarked locations where her parents and grandparents were laid to rest. My grandmother's grave and that of her deceased son, Buggs, were clearly marked with tombstones. These were much easier to identify. I paced and pondered. I again stared tentatively at each old gravesite. I strode carefully in different directions, measuring distances with the slippers on my feet. Then I chose a peaceful spot where we would finally lay Mass Pet's body. It was under a beautiful, blooming poinciana tree facing Jackson's Bay. I thought, "My beloved Mass Pet will be happy here. When the wind blows from the east, he may even be able to smell the fresh, blue Caribbean Sea."

That afternoon, Clinton and Dahlia arrived from America. Their children and mine also arrived to grieve and share in the painful ritual of Mass Pet's sendoff. We had dinner together in Mass Pet's favorite room of the house. This was the room where he cut and shaved his fresh homegrown tobacco, on the antique mahogany British Colonial table. Our father's scent permeated the room — we felt close to him. I tearfully recapped the events of his passing to the newly arrived family members. We wept, held hands, and tried to console each other. This time, we were much too distraught to begin any lamenting about the good times. As we instinctively drowned ourselves in sorrow, I wondered whether the pain would ever subside.

The next morning, a loud clanging on Twickenham's iron gates abruptly awakened us. All four gravediggers had arrived with shovels in hand or across shoulders. Clinton and I walked them to the gravesite and issued clear directions. They eagerly began to work on Mass Pet's new resting place under the shade of the old poinciana tree. After breakfast, Betty fired up the old wood-burning stove in the backyard. I reminisced about when Mass Pet lovingly built that stove. Now Betty was preparing pots full of ackee and salted cod, dumplings and boiled bananas on that old family "treasure."

In addition to paying the gravediggers, one was also expected to feed them and to provide them with an endless supply of 190-proof Jamaican white rum. I thought, "Why the hell do we have to pay, feed and booze them up at the same time?" But I was much too distraught to make waves or fight any battles. So I surrendered to the ritual and thought, "Poor bastards. I might also need to shock my own liver into submission if I had to dig graves with rusty, old shovels for a living."

They dug with those old shovels, vigorously flung dirt around, bantered away at each other in Patois, and drank the white rum all day. And at the end of each day, we visited the site to check how they were progressing. They looked up at us from that gaping hole in the ground, eyes red, dirt all over their tattered, old clothes and in their hair and nostrils. Then they'd give us a loud and drunken progress update. Any inclination to feel sorry for them and their pathetic lives was shot to smithereens, as our questions were greeted with big attitudes, more white rum requests, and the smell of weed. The poor bastards had also been smoking ganja (marijuana) on the job. Still, I was much too grief stricken to fight this battle.

On the final evening of grave digging, we strolled through Twickenham from the old poinciana tree to

Mass Pet's house. I reflected on the many times as a child I would scamper up each tropical fruit tree we passed by, filling my belly with nothing but ripe and succulent fruit. Clinton commented as we walked under one of the big sweetsop trees, "Miss Olivia, remember how we would climb this tree and hunt around for the ripest sweetsops? Those were the ones that the birds had already started to peck."

"Yeah, those were the ripest and sweetest ones," I responded nostalgically. "The birds would always discover them before we did."

"What simple and innocent times those were. We were so happy and free of any troubles then," Clinton continued.

"Our biggest worries were about who could slurp down the most fruit and dodge Cookie's rusty soupspoon chases at the same time," I reflected.

"Boy do I miss those days! Now we're back to our roots with innocence lost, putting poor Papa into the ground so he can enjoy his final rest," Clinton commented.

We sighed and continued along the short walk to Mass Pet's house to find Betty fussing with Miss Birdie about something of little importance. As the others entered the house, I stayed behind to enjoy the beautiful tropical breezes of Mass Pet's vast backyard. It was around 5:00 p.m. I watched peacefully as the breeze rustled through the leaves of the swaying fruit trees that my father had planted with his own hands.

"Miss Olivia, your father is paying you a special visit!" Betty interrupted, a touch of mystery in her voice.

Then I immediately felt the warm, live presence of something soft, which had just landed on the calf of my right leg. I turned my head gently and glanced down. "My God," I thought, as my eyes beheld the most beautiful black butterfly perched on my calf. Both wings of the creature spanned about five inches, and they were spread gently around my calf. A chill shot up my spine. I was completely mesmerized.

At that moment my mind rewound and wrapped itself around the following memory. I was eight years old. Mass Pet was home on a sabbatical from one of his European adventures. I ran home from school in tears. He reached his arms out to me and gently asked, "Miss Olivia, what's wrong? Why do you cry so sadly? Tell me, my daughter."

"They're teasing me at school again, Papa," I said, looking up at him and sobbing. "The other girls are calling me 'big-calf Olivia.' When will the rest of my body catch up with my calves, Papa? They are saying that every other part of me is skinny except for my calves. Why are they so cruel, Papa?"

Mass Pet bent over, held me tenderly by the shoulders, looked deeply into my eyes, and consoled,

"Look at your Papa, Miss Olivia. You have beautiful calves. The other girls are of no importance, my daughter."

I stopped crying, as he continued. "I promise you this: that little body will soon catch up with those gorgeous calves. Then your poor Papa will have to beat the boys away from Twickenham like a caveman wielding a big, old club."

I wiped my eyes and giggled. He continued, "The other girls are just jealous because you are a budding beauty. Trust me on that one, Miss Olivia!"

Then pretty soon he had me rolling in the grass with laughter as he changed my mood with a barrage of tickles.

I returned suddenly to the present, reached over, and touched the wing of the black butterfly spread-eagled across my calf. It gracefully flew away. I stared with peaceful wonder as it performed an awesome dance through the fruit trees nearby. Now I was ready to say goodbye to my loving father.

There is a myth about this in Jamaica. It says that when a loved one dies, he comes back to the family in the form of a black butterfly. Jamaicans call it a black bat. They treat it with respect and curiosity, mixed together with a little fear and trepidation. The black butterfly usually arrives and remains in the home of the diseased for several days after that person dies. It will fly from one room to the other and appear on a wall at the most curious of times. When my brother Lancie died, a black butterfly performed the same ritual in our home. I remember it flying around as if performing a ritualistic dance, from one room to the next, during my brother's wake.

I had indeed returned to my heritage. I was beginning to believe, with an endearing suspicion, that Mass Pet had just visited me. I knew that he would stay with us at Twickenham until we returned to America. I curiously recalled that there was no black butterfly in the house when we buried my brother Maxie. My thoughts had me justifying this. Maxie died in America, he had never lived at Twickenham, and hence his spirit was not likely to appear there.

Two days later, we laid Mass Pet to rest in peace and with much love. The service was held at Sedith's old church, with a preacher far less cantankerous than Parson Mitchell officiating. As we sang hymns at sunset over his final resting place under the old poinciana tree, I reflected on our family's perpetual fight for Twickenham. We battled against both enslavement and criminal elements. From the forefathers to our generation, we fought ferociously. I thought that inevitably if my generation of Jennings was lucky, life would end for all of us with a bitter-sweet sendoff like the one Mass Pet just got. A precious goodbye would come, with our children and grandchildren expressing unending love, compassion, and absolutely no regrets.

The black butterfly stayed perched in the hallway of Mass Pet's house, directly over the door jam to what had become Miss Birdie's bedroom. We spent the next several days after Mass Pet's funeral taking care of his personal affairs, ensuring that Miss Birdie would be able to cope, and that Betty was happy and around to take care of her. The night before our departure for America, after Dahlia and I had a final chat with Miss Birdie and put her to bed, we exited her bedroom. After noting that the black butterfly had stubbornly maintained its position above her bedroom door, Dahlia commented, "There he is ... Mass Pet continues to watch over his beloved Miss Birdie."

Dahlia and I were sharing one of the bedrooms next to Mass Pet's favorite cigar-indulging room. We closed our bedroom door and got into bed, staring blankly at the television for about an hour. I turned the television off, we said our goodnights, and were about to retire and mentally prepare for the airplane ride back to America the next day. I suddenly heard wings flapping on the wall above our bed. I remained still, opened my eyes, and looked around. There was a bright tropical moon glowing right outside of our glass jalousie window. On the wall above, I beheld the shadow of the black butterfly, gently perching itself above our heads. Dahlia touched my hand and whispered, "It's Papa. He's here to get close and connect with us for the last time. He will always be with us, Miss Olivia."

With that as a wonderful possibility, I fell into the deepest, emotionally exhausted, and most peaceful sleep I'd had in a very long time.

The next several months after my return to America were brutal. I buried myself into my stressful corporate job by day and struggled to find sleep and peace at night. I missed Mass Pet with an intense passion, and the pain of also losing Maxie overwhelmed my soul. I tried everything to ease the agony. Finally, I began going through the belongings I had taken from Twickenham and found three pairs of my father's soft cotton pajamas. I put on the blue-and-white pair that Mass Pet would wear on nights when the moon was shining at its brightest. He would stroll contentedly through the tropical fruit trees he'd single-handedly planted in the backyard. After that, he would sit on the back veranda, then he would take a few puffs of one of his freshly rolled cigars before retiring for the night. The pajamas hung loosely on my slender frame. I had to roll both sleeves and pant legs up, but that night I slept like a baby. I wore Mass Pet's pajamas several nights each week — and this not only made me feel connected to him, it also gave me peace and comfort.

By now it was the beginning of September. The pain and grief, while still intense, was becoming a little less gut wrenching. On September 11 of the same year, I was at work when a colleague bolted into my office wide-eyed and terrified, muttering something about airplanes flying into New York's World Trade Center. I rushed to the staff lounge to behold that horrible tragedy unfolding. New Yorkers fled in terror from smoke, dust and fire, as the buildings collapsed into ashes behind them. For months, this horrible tragedy was repeatedly played out on American television. The horror of that day defrayed some of my personal grief, but replaced it with fear, dread and disbelief. Within a mere few months, I had experienced deep personal agony and loss, as well as terrifying social and international wretchedness — and the anguish was not about to end.

A mere three months later I received a phone call from my daughter Charlene. She informed me that Miss Birdie had left this Earth to join Mass Pet. Again, an agonizing numbness took me over as she explained the following. My son Christopher, who had been working in his father's business in Kingston, had driven to Twickenham with his father to check on Miss Birdie's wellbeing.

"Mom, Christopher and Dad didn't like the way Miss Birdie was looking," explained Charlene. "Betty told them that she was recovering from a stomach virus. She was treated for the virus at Lionel Town hospital and sent home."

By now I was staring blankly at my bedroom walls in shock. Charlene continued, "Christopher and Dad put her in the backseat of the car and rushed her back to the same hospital. While Dad was checking her in, Christopher saw her eyes roll over into the back of her head. He yelled for the doctor. As they rushed her into the emergency room, she died."

I could utter not one single word as I heard Charlene comment, "Mom, you know that she lost the will to live after Mass Pet died. He was the love of her life. We think she just gave up and surrendered to the virus, so she could join the beloved husband she'd loved and nurtured for 54 years. Mom are you there ... Mom?"

So we flew back to Jamaica on December 26, 2001 to bury yet another beloved family member. Miss Birdie had always wanted to return to her favorite place, which was Port Royal. She never forgave Mass Pet for moving her to Twickenham, so far from her birth place in Kingston, and from her beloved Port Royal where she had spent most of her youth. It was a difficult decision to separate her in death from our father; but we buried her in her own family's burial ground next to her loving son Maxie, in the cemetery by the sea. All this, after another mournful service in the church where Captain Morgan was buried.

I had an out-of-body experience when we buried Miss Birdie. The three deaths were so close and so overwhelming, my emotions completely shut down. Like a robot with no feeling, I worked with the family to carefully plan my mother's funeral. I stood over Miss Birdie's grave, my feet buried in the sand at the cemetery by the sea. All I could do was rock to and fro as we sang the chorus of one hymn after the other. My eyes were dry, and my heart was empty. Looking back, this was my body's way of helping me cope and preventing me from just totally falling apart.

New Year's Eve that year found us in the family home at Twickenham going through the belongings of both Mass Pet and Miss Birdie. We embarked on the difficult task of deciding what to keep and what to give to Betty and other needy residents of Portland Cottage. At around 11:00 p.m., we piled into the car and drove through town, just to take a break from the pain. We spotted a street vendor stirring a big pot of fresh fish soup. We sat on the sidewalk next to him and consumed bowls of what tasted like comfort food. Then we returned to Twickenham to complete our traumatic task. We brought in the New Year close to the spirits of our beloved parents, Mass Pet and Miss Birdie.

In just nine months, we had buried our brother Maxie and mourned the loss of one entire generation of Jennings family members. When I returned to America after Miss Birdie's burial, my boss took one look at me and suggested that I take some more time off. My response was that hard work was my best release right now. I said that I would let her know when the pain and grief finally overcame my very being. Three months later, I was forced to pull off the road on my way home from work, as blinding tears began to gush from me like a crested river, flowing rapidly through my eyes, and drenching my heart. I took a two-week sabbatical, sailed to the Bahamas, and began writing this book.

chapter 16

Reflections, Challenges and Love

*S*OME OF US ARE STRONG ENOUGH TO survive discord, death and life's other challenges without emotional damage. Those of us who can confront them with courage and little or no regrets are even more fortunate.

Coping with life's challenges after the loss of my beloved Mass Pet, Miss Birdie and Maxie was indeed a struggle. Mass Pet's cotton pajamas continued to hang onto my petite frame for several months. I was now wondering whether any sense of normalcy could be felt again, let alone joy and laughter. I was sad and tormented. And though I missed them all, one memory taunted me relentlessly. Holding my beloved father in my arms as he departed this Earth was a painful thought that I could not remove from my psyche.

Clinton and Dahlia were having their own difficulties coping with their grief. So we commiserated by phone in search of support and comfort. During one phone conversation I painfully lamented.

"I don't know about you, but I feel like an orphan. No longer will we be able to board an airplane, and then fight the treacherous Jamaican traffic through Kingston to Spanish Town and Old Harbour to finally drive through Twickenham's gates with excitement in our bellies, as Mass Pet greets us with his loving hugs, welcoming smiles, and a big basket of tropical fruit. I used to feel such solace during these trips."

"Remember when we finally got to Old Harbour, how I would skillfully weave the car in and out of country bodies bustling about in the streets, passionately searching for cassavas, yams and pumpkins for their families' tables?" Clinton said, truly attempting to stay composed.

"Yes," I interrupted nostalgically. "And my foot would be piercing a hole in the floor of the car as the backseat driver in me repeatedly tried to apply its own brakes. I was a nervous wreck. My brother, I thought for sure that you'd run one of those poor housewives over."

"Ha, I was skillful, wasn't I? Then we would look ahead to behold smoke rising gracefully above a small mob of shoppers on the sidewalk,"

Clinton continued.

"Yes, and you, my brother, would pump the brakes with such urgency, our bodies would be flung forward," Dahlia chimed in, fighting her own tears with what sounded like a weak smile.

"Ah yes. But then our noses would be suddenly aroused by an incredible aroma," Clinton continued. "We were consumed by a bouquet of flavors from the most succulent jerk chicken and roast yam anyone has ever sniffed. It came from a crude sidewalk rotisserie made from an old molasses barrel. And don't forget that it was always operated by the most ornery old Rastafarian in Old Harbour."

"Then we would bolt out of the rental car," I recanted, my own eyes beading up with tears. "And like a bunch of local hooligans, we would jockey for position, elbowing competitors, and cussing away in Patois. Why all this uncouth behavior? Just so that we could get our share of the Rasta Man's delicious street corner cuisine!"

"Do you remember the looks on our faces as we 'groaned and aahed' with sheer pleasure as the taste and aroma of that incredibly spicy chicken reached our lips and hungrily tickled our Caribbean taste buds?" Dahlia chimed in. "We were always ravenous for a taste of home while living in America. And boy, this was the perfect way to satisfy that savage yearning."

"You better believe it!" Clinton continued.

"We would wash things down with an ice-cold ginger beer, while licking our fingers with sheer delight. Then we'd jump back in the car to bob and weave through more of the outrageous traffic that dangerously took us to Twickenham. As I put the pedal to the metal on the left-hand side of that country road, I would secretly dread being forced into the bushes again as car after car came barreling down on us, in another hair-raising yet successful attempt to overtake a slow-moving donkey cart."

"Now you tell us!" I commented jokingly. "And here we felt so safe with you at the controls, when all that time you were sweating bullets."

"I know it," Dahlia added. "But before that, while you were busy licking your fingers after the jerk-chicken feast, Olivia and I would slip into the local bakery across the street. There we bought bags of hot, hard-dough bread, steaming and spicy beef patties fresh out of the oven, jam rolls and raisin breads. We knew that these goodies would add to Mass Pet's and Miss Birdie's glee as we opened the big iron gates of Twickenham and rolled the car up to their beautiful and welcoming veranda!"

"And during the next several days Mass Pet would listen closely to all of our stories," I continued to wax nostalgically. "Then he would comfort and advise us how to face life's challenges as immigrants living in America. He would always say, 'Miss Olivia, life is a battle and to survive you must continue the fight.'"

"But Papa," I'd respond, "When does the battle become less brutal?"

"All will be well, Miss Olivia," he'd placate with a few gentle hugs. "Just forge ahead and don't let them see you sweat. You only look back when you come to see your old Papa in Portland Cottage."

"Then I would feel my body and mind slow down," I continued. "And I would begin to blend in with the warm caress of the balmy tropical breeze that brushed the fruit trees over our heads. Ah, this really was home. And with Mass Pet there, it was my refuge, my solace and my comfort."

Clinton sighed deeply as we shared more coping stories with one another. Dahlia read her Bible and prayed. Clinton put in extra hours at work to dull the pain. I did the same and continued to wear Mass pet's cotton pajamas to bed.

Grief counseling was a company benefit that I took advantage of at my boss' prodding. There I learned that wearing Mass Pet's cotton pajamas was a healthy part of the grieving process. It helped keep me connected with my beloved father, according to the counselor.

She also counseled, "Olivia, it takes an average of two years for us to grieve one loss. You have suffered three losses in a short nine-month period. Do not be in a hurry to recover from this devastation. It will take a good six years for the pain to significantly subside."

"Really?" I exclaimed. "You mean I'll be feeling like this for six years?"

"No, the pain will get less intense over time; but now that you know this, allow yourself to cry when the tears start to rush from your heart. If you are driving in heavy traffic when they begin to blind you, pull over, and cry your eyes out. It's all part of the healing process."

Uncontrollable tears indeed. I pulled my car over a few times while heading home from work and just let the tears rip. She was right, letting it out was one of the greatest ways to fortify my wounded soul.

In one of our three-way conversations, my siblings and I decided on the following, "Let's stay closer together even though we live in different parts of the country. And let us have a family reunion at least every two years."

"How about also selling Mass Pet's house with only two acres of land," I suggested. "We could, of course, continue to maintain Twickenham."

"That's a good idea, Miss Olivia," Clinton chimed in.

"We could use the money from the sale to buy a villa on the beach in Ocho Rios or Montego Bay," I continued, feeling excitement for the first time in almost a year. "We could hold our family reunions there."

"That may be a hard decision for us to make right now. Maybe later on when the pain subsides?"

Dahlia commented, unable to get past her emotions.

"That would be a painful move," Clinton responded, after thinking for a moment. "But you know, it may be a better choice than to have strangers living in Mass Pet's house."

"Yes," I added. "You know that we rented the house just to have a presence there and to keep squatters away. And Mass Pet always told us to sell the house after he died. We would disregard his words, because the thought of losing him was much too devastating."

For weeks after this conversation, I reflected deeply on my own life's journey. My guess is that losing one's parents opens the floodgates to reflections, evaluations, and sometimes even regret; but for me there were no regrets. I had been there for my loved ones during the good times as well as the bad. I had worked with my siblings to ensure that Mass Pet and Miss Birdie received the best care available to them in their final years.

Reflections now had me thinking about how strong I had become as a woman, a mother, a daughter, an auntie and a friend. I had chosen single parenting over an unhappy marriage. I fought relentlessly to ensure that my children had balance, dignity, and the will and determination to survive life's adversities with their heads held high. And I was tired but I kept going.

After 10 years of single parenting, I was recruited

up to Atlanta, Georgia, as human resources director of a dynamic and well-known minority women's college. I had painfully and reluctantly sent my two younger children to Jamaica so they could finish high school there under the British system. Besides, their father and I also wanted them to fully experience their West Indian culture. This was in their best interest, I told myself. The decision caused unbearable pain; but the fact that they were with their father and close to grandparents from both sides who kept tabs on them, gave me some comfort. And assuming the role of "fun parent" who had them to spoil and pamper on holidays and summer breaks definitely came with its own appeal.

So here I was, alone in a new American city, blazing more trails with my usual determined and adventuresome spirit. All this under the strength gained from Mass Pet's advice, "Life is a battle, Miss Olivia." Work life at the college was both challenging and affirming. I spent many evenings at the art gallery or soaking up lectures given by famous African-American scholars. I also joyfully looked on as well-known Hollywood personalities visited the campus. One came to teach a summer class. The other came to oversee a philanthropic project or to visit his child who was a student at the college.

Yet the evenings at home were lonesome. So after accepting an invitation to give a talk at one of the Atlanta-Jamaica Association meetings, I ventured out to find familiar territory. And one Saturday night in early August, I dressed in an outfit that hugged all curves, arrived without escort at the Jamaican Independence dance, and was aggressively pursued by a handsome and prominent Jamaican dentist.

As I floated through the room introducing myself to others, he tapped me on the shoulder and crooned, "May I have the pleasure of this dance with the most beautiful woman in the room?"

"Sure, if you promise to behave yourself!" I turned around and playfully responded.

We slow danced for a few minutes. Then he looked me straight in the eyes and boldly announced, "You may not realize this, but you are going to be my wife!"

I threw my head back, laughed out loud, and shot back. "Not in this lifetime ... not unless you drag me to the church kicking and screaming!"

The damn dentist was right. Two years later after a loving courtship, we were married by Jamaica's chief religious figure. I was dragged to the church once more — and there was some kicking, but not too much screaming. The reception was held in a gorgeous ocean-side villa named Cirrhosis by the Sea on Jamaica's North Coast. It was intimate and magical. I looked forward to a life filled with love and to having a lifelong partner.

But love and adventure soon became struggle and

dissent. Emotionally and financially draining —
these were the words that best described my second
marriage. After five years of attempting to make the
relationship work, my husband announced that he
now wanted us to adopt newborn babies.

Well, this time it was not youth and domestic
doldrums that made me do it. It was marital and
financial distress, mixed with sheer terror. I was
terrified at the thought of potentially raising teenagers
in my fifties, in a relationship with a man who simply
did not have it together. So the decision to pull foot,
like the ancestors in slavery put it — though gut
wrenching — was imminent. We lived together in our
large Atlanta home for one year before the divorce
became final, with me upstairs in the master suite,
and my now-ex husband downstairs in the suite next
to our pool and gym. We were quiet and sad, but we
remained respectful of each other's space.

One month before the divorce became final
my daughter Charlene flew up from Florida for
Thanksgiving. She knew that I would be alone
for the holidays. My soon-to-be ex-husband was
heading to Jamaica for the holiday weekend. My
son Christopher and younger daughter Tanya, both
in college, were also heading to Jamaica to spend
the weekend with their father.

Charlene had recently received an honorable
discharge from the U.S. Air Force. South Florida
was now her home, and she was successfully

holding down an exciting position in the hotel industry. I was very grateful that my first-born was now in safer surroundings. Several years earlier I was sent a copy of her Will, as the Air Force prepared to dispatch her straight into the Gulf War — that war ended one week prior to her departure to the Middle East. Needless to say, the stress and worry of seeing my child's Last Will and Testament had almost put me away for good.

But the ancestors continued to watch out for me. Charlene and I prepared and consumed a delicious Jamaican Thanksgiving dinner in the beautiful home in which I was now spending some of my loneliest days.

"Mom, chin up! Let's go out for a night on the town," she urged, eyes bright and full of mischief. "Where is there a good place for us to go dancing in this God-forsaken town?"

"Oh, I don't know my daughter," I responded reluctantly. "You know how much I love to dance; but I just cannot muster up the enthusiasm these days."

"Oh come on!" My colorful and exuberant daughter exclaimed. "Where is that youthful mother I know, with the killer face and body, who dances up a storm to blow off steam?"

So soon we were strolling into a hot salsa nightclub in Buckhead looking like sisters out on the prowl. We were turning heads all the way. After one drink I had forgotten most of my troubles. As my body swayed to the infectious Latin rhythms, I looked up at an equally compelling voice above me declaring, "Don't you look beautiful tonight. Are you both sisters?"

"Thanks for the lovely compliment," I responded.

"Damn!" I thought. "He's like a tall, cool drink of water … and so handsome." But I kept my cool and continued, "I'm Olivia, and allow me to introduce you to my daughter, Charlene."

After reaching across the table to shake Charlene's hand, he continued with that Latin charm that almost brought me to my knees one other time in the past. Different man, same charm.

"And who is the lucky man responsible for that beautiful smile of yours — your husband?"

"Yes, I believe it is!" I responded, now playful and smiling with mischief.

I could see the disappointment in his face as he attempted to keep his own cool. So I continued playing the game of cat and mouse.

"He is a dentist, and he definitely brightened my smile by working on these pearly white teeth of mine!"

We both shook with laughter. I couldn't help but notice his pearly whites too. His name was John Vierra. We danced the night away while Charlene enjoyed a pulsating meringue with one admirer after the other.

I had been silently planning a much-anticipated return to South Florida after my divorce. And coincidentally, John had just taken an early retirement from a 23-year job with a major firm. He recently bought a townhouse in Ft. Lauderdale and was packing up to move there in the next few weeks. We promised to stay in touch and get together when I arrived.

With an amazing leap of fate, in one week I made a series of previously planned moves that changed my life significantly. I walked alone into Atlanta's downtown courthouse whispering the Twenty-Third Psalm. Then I sat in front of the judge with my attorney and listened closely as he granted my divorce. This was on Tuesday. The next day I accepted an offer to buy the beautiful home where loneliness had become my best friend. And on Thursday, I resigned from my job.

Freedom and liberation — how sweet it was! The door was now open, and I was ready to rush through it with outstretched arms. Without one degree of animosity, I hugged my ex-husband goodbye and wished him a good life. Then I got into my convertible that was packed solid with some of life's necessities and headed south-of-the-border toward Ft. Lauderdale.

But about two hours from the Florida border I escaped near death. I was cruising along at 75 mph in the left lane of the highway when there it was, an eight-foot sheet of aluminum, airborne and flying straight toward my car. It headed directly at my face from a pick-up truck that noisily roared by. I swerved onto the left shoulder of the road as the "missile" cut a hole in the right side of my convertible top, scratched past my two right windows, and tore off my antenna.

As I pulled over so did the other driver; but he was obviously more interested in retrieving the deadly weapon that had almost decapitated me. I beckoned to him, and he lumbered over to me red-faced from the distance. The man was about 350 pounds of toughness. So I was again whispering the Twenty-Third Psalm. Two hours later after the police did their work, I continued on my trip to Ft. Lauderdale, still shaken, and now whispering the Twenty-Seventh Psalm. The reality of my divorce had quickly set in. I no longer had a husband to rescue me. So I reminded myself, "You're a big girl Olivia and you're on your own again. Deal with life's challenges and keep on moving. Chin up! No looking back! Life is a battle."

I arrived at Charlene's Ft. Lauderdale apartment seven hours later.

"My God Mom, we'll need to fatten you up," my daughter laughingly observed after giving me the once over. "How much do you weigh now after worrying about the damn divorce and everything else that's been going on?"

"Your girl is a solid 96 pounds, thank you very much!" I replied, flexing a puny right muscle.

When Charlene responded by giving me one of her big, warm hugs, I immediately knew that the healing had begun. My beloved daughter had me laughing with pure glee at night after she arrived home from work. Then she took me to the Jamaican side of town to buy fresh natural shakes and other Caribbean roots drinks in her attempt to "fatten me up." This was her idea of nurturing Mom — and it was working. On Mother's Day, she dragged me to an erotic café on South Beach where we ate, drank and "salsa'd" our behinds off to the Latin rhythms of the night. There was fun in my life again.

John Vierra soon came calling, and we eventually became best friends. Then we became a couple. He'd invite me over on weekends. And being the great gourmet cook that he was, I had no problem with eagerly devouring his comforting Domincan soups and other exotic dishes. That was John's version of nurturing, and I soaked it up.

At his prodding, we'd pack picnic baskets with his cuisine of the day. Then we'd relax and bask on Hollywood Beach for hours, watch the sun go down, while talking about life, politics and world events. Though not as educated as me, John was witty, intelligent and humorous. We soon developed a very strong bond. And with foresight and some resolve, I took a second-level executive position in my field, while pledging to give myself more work-life balance.

In August a few years later, I hosted our first Jennings family reunion at my lake home in Florida. During this reprieve, we prepared sumptuous meals together, played games into the wee hours of the morning, and picnicked and cavorted on the beach. We also took a boat ride on the inter-coastal waterway so we could dine and watch a live show on a private island under the warm-and-balmy Florida skies. We reflected and bonded as a family, enjoyed ourselves for the first time in years, and vowed to do reunions at least every two years.

I've been told that ambition, independence and strength are among my better attributes; but while recent family trauma had almost pounded me into submission, they also awakened my drive to fully explore my creative and entrepreneurial sides.

With my children grown, I was now free to pursue some of my passions, though I continued to work in a demanding corporate environment. So I began taking trips to the Caribbean, all by myself. Once there, I detached from life's routines, listened to reggae, salsa music and Jamaican folk songs, and pursued the burning passion of finishing my novel. When a downturn in the American stock market ate away at a significant portion of my short-term investments, I took my losses on the chin and entered the real estate investment market.

Two of my properties were on the beach. So not only was I expressing my creativity through writing, I also interior designed my beach condos so they could be easily rented. I monitored the booming Florida real estate market very closely, exited the condo market two years later, and began exploring other real estate possibilities.

I had succeeded in filling my life with rewarding moneymaking ventures, but had neglected my romantic life. I claimed to be burned out on men with their egos and insecurities. By then, John Viera had become an unpleasant memory. He moved on to a young girl 30 years his junior, because of his need to "mold her" into what he wanted.

"You intimidate me," he claimed. "You are too driven and independent! You don't need me."

I wondered when the idiot would learn that though a woman may not need financial support, she still needed a man for companionship, nurturing and emotional sustenance. The young girl would soon be boasting both pregnancy and subtle control over "poor old John."

"Aaah, people eventually got what they deserve," I thought. "But why, oh why, does it take so long for them to get what's coming to them?"

Then one afternoon a girlfriend called with an invitation that ended up putting some zest back into my personal life.

"Olivia, tomorrow evening the Caribbean Bar

Association is hosting their annual cocktail party," she announced. "It's being held at a great hotel in downtown Hollywood. Meet me there after work at around 6:30 p.m., and I won't take no for an answer."

"OK girl, but are there going to be a bunch of obnoxious and egotistical lawyers there?" I questioned with cynicism.

"Don't even go there!" she impatiently reprimanded. "You have not been out of that house of yours socially in a long time. And I don't know what you're saving yourself for. Let's just go to the party and have a good time."

"But what kind of people will be there?" I insisted.

"That doesn't matter. They have this event every year, and there's usually great food and good music. I'll see you there at 6:30 — and wear one of those great outfits of yours, will you? Geez, you're becoming boring!"

So I showed up at 6:30 p.m. after a harrowing day at the office, skeptically hoping that I would not be wasting my time lollygagging with a bunch of jerks.

I glanced around the room, but my girlfriend was nowhere to be found. So after grumbling and sighing, I strolled outside and plopped down under a quaint and inviting Tiki hut by the pool. "A glass of wine will soothe my frazzled nerves," I thought. Then I began focusing on the charming one-man band that was making a bold attempt to play authentic Caribbean tunes nearby.

"Don't even think about it!" I silently warned myself as my eyes moved behind the bar to behold the gorgeous young bartender walking flirtatiously toward me. Look at him, prancing around in tropical shorts and shirt showing off a tattoo, great chest, and muscles that would make a woman tremble. Then more self-talk, "He's probably one hell of a player, so you'd better keep your drawers up and stay the hell away from him." I was actually beginning to convince myself.

My thoughts were abruptly interrupted as he strutted up to me with that innocent baby face, adorned with a huge smile. The front of his loud red-and-white flowered shirt was wide open. The chest was bulging and chiseled.

"You are absolutely stunning," he crooned. "My name is Nick, and where may I ask are you from?"

Now I was struggling to figure out the accent. I was puzzled. He looked West Indian, with shoulder-length and neatly cropped dreadlocks; but there was something very unique and intriguing about him.

"Thank you. I'm Olivia Jennings and to answer your question, I'm Jamaican."

"Really! My parents are also Jamaican but I was born and raised in Europe. Austria to be exact," he smiled. Now the charm was really beginning to hurt my eyes and ears.

With some trepidation, I'm now thinking what an amazing combination this was. My heart said, "A European who looks like a Jamaican — Lord, why are you tempting me? I just stopped by to have a drink and wait patiently for my girlfriend. Why do I have to run into the likes of him?"

Then I was forced to refocus, because he was now staring deeply into my eyes. I immediately began thinking trash; I wonder if he makes love like a European too?

"Don't even think about it!" my wise-and-sober side kept scolding away relentlessly.

"Olivia, would you like a body shot?" Again, this muscular young creature interrupted my private scolding.

OK. It had been awhile since I'd stepped out on the town so I didn't know what the hell a body shot was. And before my mind could begin conjuring up any erotic interpretations, I asked, "What, in God's name, may I ask is that?"

Now I had asked for it. The hunk mischievously began to demonstrate. It was a shot of liquor that he would stick into his waistband. And I'd be required to skillfully slurp it down while getting dangerously close to the six-pack of a stomach he was sporting. After again quieting the very sober and innocent angel on my shoulder nagging "don't even think about it," I let out a sigh, and one hell-of-a blush took over my body.

"Another glass of White Zinfandel will do just fine. But thanks for that tempting offer," I mumbled.

"Coming right up; but only after you promise to give me your phone number!" he replied — and there was naughtiness now in his eyes.

"I'll give you my business card. Now get me the wine, will you?" I smiled and curtly replied.

As he approached me with the wine and a piece of paper, he crooned, "Great, and by the way, here's my phone number. Call me anytime, promise?"

After this flirtatious first encounter, Nick's phone calls would break up my day at work, with short yet pleasant and stimulating conversations. His invitations for a date would consistently be met with, "Let me get back to you on that."

Although our conversations did ease my mind about his being a "player," I was now concerned about the difference in our ages. Yet all fears can always be assuaged. One Friday after a particularly exhausting week, Nick again called. And this time he asked, "Didn't I give you my phone number when we met a couple of months ago?"

"Yes, I believe you did … so?" This was my coy reply, which was met with the response: "You're not using it! How about meeting me at the Keg, a wonderful British pub in Dania Beach? They have great steak and kidney pies, and the Guinness Stout keeps flowing all night. Don't say 'no' this time, *please*," he pleaded.

So I did a preemptive strike on the nagging angel on my shoulder who was now beginning to get on my last nerve and said, "OK, he's sweet and gorgeous. And I'm tired and vulnerable. This young man has pursued me for two months. I'm going out with him, so don't even think about it!"

I met Nick at the Keg, and the rest is history. We ate, drank, played a spirited game of darts, and like Miss Birdie used to say, "Fan me with a brick," but I had a great time. And the chemistry between us was really intense. In the midst of all this hanging out, I heard a wonderful song playing on the jukebox.

"Who is that?" I asked. "What a great rhythm. Don't think I've heard that song before."

"That's me, Olivia," Nick casually replied as he skillfully threw a dart.

"Yeah, right." I quickly responded, trying to throw a more precise dart then he just did. "Come on, tell me who is really singing that song? I'd like to buy the CD."

He gently took me by the hand, walked me over to the jukebox, and then he began flipping through the CDs. And there he was on one of the CD covers, gorgeous pose, stage name, dreadlocks flowing.

"Why didn't you tell me that you are a musician?" I asked, now a bit puzzled.

"Because gorgeous," he looked me straight in the

eyes and replied. "I thought you might not want to go out with me if you thought I was just some old bartender."

So Nick and I became an item after our first date. Tenuous attempts on my part to get opinions from my daughters Charlene and Tanya about my dating a younger man were met with, "You go girl! You only live once so enjoy the ride and get your groove on, Mom!"

After eyeing Nick suspiciously for a while, my son Christopher finally gave in and became buddies with my new, gorgeous European-Jamaican suitor with the dreadlocks; but not before reminding me about the tantrum I threw earlier when he, "my dear son," grew his own dreadlocks at age 19. Life had truly gotten to be exciting and humorous.

Then the hurricanes hit South Florida. Four of them ... one after the other. By the time hurricane number three rolled around, I put the shutters up at home and headed for the nearest shelter. Taunting us, Hurricane Francis lingered off the Florida coastline for two full days.

That year I had decided to brave hurricane Ivan at home, with shutters up and nerves frayed. Ivan was hurricane number four of the season. It was heading straight for Jamaica before potentially hitting South Florida. So I called William, the live-in caretaker of Mass Pet's home at Twickenham. I wanted to ensure that he prepared the house for the arrival of our unwelcome guest. And then something strange happened — that night after falling into a deep sleep, Mass Pet's musky body scent had eerily permeated my bedroom. Without a doubt, his presence was with me in that room in my Florida home and goosebumps took over my entire body. I awakened, turned the light on, and glanced around for the black butterfly. It was nowhere in sight.

Then I turned the television on to behold hurricane Ivan hovering along the coastline of Portland Cottage's peninsula. Though Jamaica was not going to take a direct hit, the devastation was imminent. And as I tried to stay calm, there on TV was Terry, the granddaughter of one of Mass Pet's best friends Joe, wet and weeping as the reporter interviewed her.

"A 20-foot wave came ashore from nearby Barnswell Beach, and everyone living on the Salt Pond had their homes washed away," Terry recounted through tears. "We had our two boys in our arms when the wave hit us!" Terry told the reporter, wet and hysterical. Her husband looked on, terror in his eyes.

"The wave was so big, it swept my two-year old right out of my arms," she exclaimed, weeping hysterically. Then Terry babbled on about trying to hold onto a tree with one hand and her baby with the other. But Ivan's vengeance took her baby away for good, she screamed. Totally terrified, I looked on, realizing that this was the reason for Mass Pet's earlier "visit."

For an entire week, I called Jamaica but to no avail. The phone lines were either down or busy. Finally, a call came through from William.

"Miss Jennings, the entire roof of Mass Pet's house is gone," he babbled nervously.

"Oh my God, William. Are you OK?" I interrupted, scared to death.

"Yes Maam, I'm OK." William replied above loud static in the phone lines. "It began in the living room, and as I moved from one room to the next, the roof kept peeling off from the house above my head as the winds howled and roared. Miss Jennings, the room where you store the old folks' British Colonial furniture has been demolished, and the furniture has been washed away."

William caught his breath then continued, now with an amazing calm, "But Miss Jennings, that's not the worse part. Remember Mr. Mack, your grandmother's trusted friend and caretaker of Twickenham for over 50 years?"

"Of course, I remember dear old Mr. Mack! Is he all right?" I interrupted frantically.

"No Maam. The small wooden house he retired in collapsed on his head during the hurricane, and he's dead!" William replied, holding back tears.

"Oh no, William. Please don't tell me that," I painfully responded.

"And Miss Jennings, a 25-foot wave came in on us

from Barnswell Beach and killed eight people living at Salt Pond, including Mass Joe's great grandson. The poor child was washed right out of his mother's arms."

"May God rest their souls in peace," I commented. "William I'm so sorry. Where are you staying now?"

"With a cousin of mine in May Pen, Maam," William responded. Now he sounded a bit disoriented.

"William, are you still there? William?" I urged.

"Yes Maam. I lost all of my clothes when the roof peeled off the house. I don't know whether I'm coming or going."

"Don't worry William, we'll start arranging to replace the roof and I'll send you a package with some new clothes." I tried to comfort him, despite my own panic and sense of loss.

One year later, Mass Pet's home was sporting a brand new roof. But poor Mr. Mack could not be replaced. Another two years later, we were again replacing the roof of Mass Pet's house. This time, it was hurricane Wilma that once again wreaked havoc in a destructive path around Portland Cottage's coastline. Now the family is talking about holding the next Jennings family reunion at Twickenham, before the forces of nature ensure that Mass Pet's house is lost forever.

And life and the generations continue to forge
ahead. I took my first-born Charlene to buy a
beautiful white-lace wedding gown made for a
princess. It was her father's role to walk her down
the aisle looking all grey-haired and distinguished;
but I am Mass Pet's daughter and part of my role
is to defy convention. So I strolled down the aisle
on the arms of my younger man, Nick, looking
gorgeous in a fitted ice-green and crystal gown
made for a queen. I looked around at my beautiful
children at the wedding. Charlene was a princess
in gorgeous white lace; Tanya was adorned in black
bustier and flowing platinum chiffon; and my son
Christopher sported an elegant black tuxedo.
I thought, "The ancestors have brought us to where
we are at this moment — and life is good indeed!"

Acknowledgements

SPECIAL ACKNOWLEDGEMENTS AND LOVE to my remarkable family, especially my father Clovis Gladstone Jennings, my brother Clifton Orlando Jennings, my sister Herma Yvonne Jennings, and my wonderful children Tara Jennings Crooks, Anthony Lancelot Jennings Crooks, and Charmaine Virginia Jennings. And to Jamaica, the amazing and exotic island of my birth and heritage.

Lastly, thank you Michelle Gamble-Risley for believing in me.

Author Acknowledgements

THE HISTORICAL EVENTS RELATED AS stories in this novel are reported to have really taken place. The strength and determination of the Maroons are a source of pride to all Jamaicans; in 1950's Cuba, Fidel Castro staged a revolution, the effects of which are still being felt, and Jamaica experienced economic and political turmoil in the 1970s.

In writing this book, there was a desire to research timelines and historical occurrences surrounding Sedith's, Aunt Suzie's and Mass Pet's stories. Therefore, the works of several authors were referenced, whom I wish to acknowledge at this time.

For Sedith's stories about the Maroons, Werner Zips' *Black Rebels* was referenced. This book was published in 1999 by Markus Wiener Publishers, New Jersey, and Ian Randle Publishers, Ltd., Jamaica.

Many thanks to John Miller, Aaron Kenedi and Andrei Codrescu whose work *Inside Cuba*, provided perspective on the contents of Aunt Suzie's letters from Cuba. *Inside Cuba* was published in 2003 by Marlowe & Company, New York.

Finally, Evelyne Huber Stephens' and John D. Stephens' *Democratic Socialism in Jamaica* was used to substantiate the information Mass Pet wrote in his letters about the Jamaican socialist experiment. This 1986 work was published in the United Kingdom by Macmillan Education Ltd.

Biography

Norma Yvonne Jennings

*N*ORMA JENNINGS WAS BORN AND RAISED on the Caribbean island of Jamaica in the West Indies. From an exotic multi-ethnic background of black, white and East Indian descent, two strong and dynamic women and a remarkably intelligent and adventurous father influenced her.

293

Ms. Jennings migrated to the United States in the early 1970s, where she earned a Bachelor of Business Administration degree from Angelo State University and graduated from the Management Development Program at Harvard Graduate School. She built a successful career as corporate executive in the hotel, education, banking and health care industries and has specialized training and experience in recruitment, employee relations, compensation, employee benefits, information technology and labor and immigration laws.

Ms. Jennings has three grown and productive children, and enjoys dual citizenship in both Jamaica and the United States. She stays close to the old estate she inherited in Jamaica, her beloved Twickenham. She is currently working on her second book.